THE CURSED MAN

KEITH ROMMEL

D1520677

SUNBURY PRESS

Mechanicsburg, Pennsylvania   USA

Published by Sunbury Press, Inc.
50 West Main Street, Suite A
Mechanicsburg, Pennsylvania 17055

www.sunburypress.com

For information about special discounts for bulk purchases, please contact Sunbury Press Orders Dept. at (855) 338-8359 or orders@sunburypress.com.

To request one of our authors for speaking engagements or book signings, please contact Sunbury Press Publicity Dept. at publicity@sunburypress.com.

ISBN: 978-1-62006-368-2 (Trade Paperback)
ISBN: 978-1-934597-98-9 (Mobipocket)
ISBN: 978-1-934597-97-2 (ePub)

THIRD SUNBURY PRESS EDITION: February 2014

Product of the United States of America
0 1 1 2 3 5 8 13 21 34 55

Set in Bookman Old Style
Designed by Lawrence Knorr
Cover by Lawrence Knorr

Front cover image: *Moundsville State Penitentiary* by Lawrence Knorr.

Continue the Enlightenment!

OTHER BOOKS BY
KEITH ROMMEL

THE LURKING MAN

THE SINFUL MAN

In memory of my father

Raymond F. Rommel

There is not a day that goes by that I don't think of you. And though time has begun to take away some of my pain, the one thing it can never take away is how deeply I love you.

I dedicate this book to my wife, Jennifer, and our children, Caitlin and Travis, who are my inspiration in everything I do.

To my family and friends: thank you for always being there.

CHAPTER 1

FINAL STRAW

The past.

Alister stood over his wife's lifeless body. "You've gotten them all. Are you happy?" he said.

She was on the bathroom floor, lying on her back. Her wide and accusing eyes were focused on him. The water that overflowed from the bathtub soaked the jeans and turtleneck sweater she wore, and they clung to her body in a farewell embrace. A razorblade that glimmered in the thick blood that painted the floor around her body held his attention.

"You bastard."

He kicked the razorblade away and fell to his knees with clenched fists.

"Oh, Sharon, please don't look at me like that." He brushed his hand lightly over her eyes to close them. A slash of pain in the pit of his stomach doubled him over, and he vomited next to her body.

"I'm sorry."

He wiped his chin and looked to words scribbled on the wall with a finger dipped in blood: *I saw it.*

He pounded his fists against the tile until flesh ripped and bone bruised. Panting like a wild animal, he glanced around the room.

"I know you're in here! Why don't you show yourself, you coward?"

The spout in the bathtub dripped and drew his attention. He shuddered at what he saw and quickly looked away. "You've crossed the line this time. Do you hear me? You've crossed the line!"

He looked at Sharon and lowered his nose to her hair in search of the familiar scent of her shampoo. He

1

pulled away, surprised by the musty stench of stagnant water mixed with blood.

He wiped his nose with the back of his hand and noticed both vertical and horizontal cuts on her wrists. The lacerations were deep and jagged.

"Oh Sharon, what did it make you do?"

Leaning his back against the toilet, he pulled Sharon's limp body into his lap. Water and blood that dripped from her clothes soaked his legs, and he focused on her face. Her purple lips were parted ever so slightly and invited one final kiss.

He tongued the cold sting the kiss left on his mouth and rocked her gently. He looked over his shoulder. "You couldn't leave them alone, could you?"

Laughter, elusive and taunting, sent a shiver up his spine. He clamped his eyes shut and slapped his hands over his ears.

"Stop it! I've had enough of you! Do you hear me? Enough of you!"

He scanned the room and slowly took his hands away.

Silence.

He lowered his wife to the floor and straightened her limbs. He neatened her wrinkled clothes and ran taut fingers through her tangled hair. "I know how you need to look presentable."

He stood and stared at the wall as he walked to the bathtub. Taking a deep breath, he tried to control his shaking limbs and fight the swirl of pain that ripped at his insides.

He looked into the bathwater. His one-year-old daughter was floating facedown. Her naked, plump body had turned a sick shade of purple, and her short blonde hair reached out in all directions as if in a desperate attempt to grab onto something.

"Becca, no!"

He gasped and held the edge of the tub to keep from falling.

"What have you done to them?"

He scooped her out of the water and held her tight. He kissed her icy cheek and squeezed her.

"Blame me for this, not your mother. It wasn't her doing."

He wiped her body clean and dry, and then wrapped her in a towel. Then he placed her next to her mother and left the bathroom. He walked out of the house.

Alister lay prone in the path of a distant vehicle that was rapidly approaching. The vision of his dead wife and child seared inside his mind's eye filled him with such agony that he had become desperate to escape it.

"Please," he said as he watched the vehicle approach, "let this end here. I can't take anymore."

It was headed straight for him.

"You know I won't let you die," a voice said. It was so loud and clear that it had to have come from his mind.

"But why?" Alister said.

"Because you invited me inside, and it is my right."

"It was a mistake. And I can't live with what I just saw!"

"It doesn't matter. I won't let you go."

"Why do I concern myself with the things you say? You're a thing from my imagination, and I'm through with you."

The sound of tires screeching pulled Alister from his reverie, and he watched as the tire stopped less than a foot away from his face. Gravel in the tread and wear that exposed the steel belt was easy to see. The smell of burnt rubber disguised the stench of death that soaked his clothing. And the heat that emanated from the engine was like the breath of a savage animal that stood over him.

"Do you still believe I am inside your mind?"

The driver of the vehicle jumped out of his car and ran to Alister's side. "Are you OK?"

Alister closed his eyes and drew a deep breath.

The man hovered over Alister, unsure what to do. "I didn't see you until the last second. I could've killed you!"

Alister felt the dull thump of his own heart. "I can only wish."

"Where are you hurt?"

"Everywhere."

"You're covered in blood." The man's hands continued to drift over Alister, but he didn't touch him. "Try not to move."

"It's not my blood," Alister said. He didn't look at the man's face because it would be another to haunt his dreams.

"I'm going to call for help."

"No, don't."

The man paused.

"My wife and daughter," Alister said.

"What?" The man moved his ear close to Alister's lips.

"They're dead." He raised an unsteady hand and extended a finger. "They are over there."

"Where?" The man looked in the direction Alister was pointing. Houses, one after the other, all looked the same. "Which one?"

"It doesn't matter. You should go before it's too late."

The man stood. "I'm calling the police." He pulled a phone from his pocket and quickly dialed. He lifted the phone to his ear and grunted.

"No, not again!" Alister said and sat up. He watched the man drop to his knees and clutch his chest. The man flopped forward, and the cell phone clattered across the pavement.

"Nine one one, what's your emergency?"

CHAPTER 2

A CONFRONTATION

Present day.

Dr. Anna Lee looked up at the three-story, gothic revival limestone structure. Steel bars covered every window, and two towers, one on either side of the large stairway, gave the impression of a well-guarded fort.

Located in the town of Binghamton, New York, Sunnyside Capable Care Mental Institution was well secluded on a one-hundred-sixty-five-acre site. Surrounded by a thick outlying forest, unoccupied dirt roads stretched to all corners of the compound.

Anna climbed twenty steep weather-stained cement steps leading to a vast air-conditioned lobby. The cool air that caressed her body demanded a groan of satisfaction. She tugged on the collar of her blouse and mopped the sweat from her brow with a handkerchief.

A dozen rows of auditorium-style seating off to her right were vacant, and a flat-screen television mounted on the wall flickered with no volume. Fifteen-foot-high ceilings exaggerated every sound, and a plump woman working on a computer behind a large semicircular desk in the back of the room went about her business without pause.

Anna moved to the desk and set the heavy briefcase she was carrying down. Its small metal feet clacked loudly against the porcelain tile floor. She cleared her throat. "Excuse me."

The woman stopped working and looked at Anna. "Yes?"

"I am Dr. Lee." She motioned to the identification tag clipped to her breast pocket. "I am here to see a patient."

"We have three 335 patients in this facility, doctor. What is the name of the patient you've come to see?"

"Alister Kunkle."

The plump woman paused and held Anna's gaze. "I'm sorry, but Mr. Kunkle isn't allowed visitors." She returned her focus to the computer screen.

"I'm not here to visit the patient. I have come to perform an evaluation of both Mr. Kunkle and the hospital on behalf of Miles Griffen and the American Psychological Association."

The woman sighed and dropped her hands onto the desktop. "I'm sorry you've made the trip here, but there are no exceptions to this rule, and you're interrupting me. I have a lot of work to do, so if you'll excuse me..."

Anna's cheeks reddened. "I don't think you seem to understand. If I don't receive this hospital's full cooperation, I can see to it that the funding is reevaluated."

The woman peered over the computer monitor. "Threats aren't necessary, doctor. It is merely protocol, and I am following the rules."

Anna unclipped her identification tag and dropped it on the keyboard. "And I am following mine. What is your name?"

"Bonnie," she said as she eyed the glossy badge with Anna's photo and job title. She compared the picture to the person that stood before her.

Anna pressed her hands on the desktop and leaned forward. "Well, Bonnie, I suggest you get off of your ass and make the necessary arrangements to get me in to see Mr. Kunkle."

Bonnie didn't question whether the person pictured was the same as the one that stood before her. She was just another state employee that had come to flex their muscles.

"I have been nothing less than courteous to you and you have been nothing less than rude to me," Anna said. "Before I get Miles Griffin on the phone, it would behoove you to get me in to see my patient."

"But there is something you should know about the man you're about to see."

"I'm sorry, I didn't realize you were qualified to give me a prognosis on the patient," Anna said. "Are you a doctor?"

"No, but—"

"Then get me inside so I can see my patient."

"But I don't think you understand."

Anna removed a cell phone from her pocket and flipped it open. "No, I don't think you understand. Last chance or it's your job."

Bonnie took Anna's identification tag and stood. "I don't have authorization to allow you access, Dr. Lee, but I will get you the director."

"Very well." She flipped her phone closed, picked up her briefcase and pointed at the seats. "I'll wait right over there. Don't keep me too long."

"I won't be gone but a minute."

Bonnie spun on her heels and entered digits on a digital keypad mounted on the wall. A buzzer sounded and she opened a door several feet from her desk. Bonnie exited the room.

Anna sat and placed the briefcase on the seat next to her. She slapped a hand over her mouth to mute a chuckle. Confrontation wasn't her strong suit, but this one she handled like a pro.

Moments later, Bonnie reentered the room with a short, thin man in tow. He wore Coke-bottle glasses, which made his eyes look big, and he had a few random strands of hair on top of an otherwise bald head. He approached Anna with an extended hand and bright smile. "Hello, Dr. Lee. I'm Director Conroy."

He had a voice like a mouse, which matched his looks perfectly.

Anna stood, took the director's hand and pumped it up and down twice. His handshake was firm, and she matched it.

"Thank you for seeing me. It seems there is some confusion. I am here to see Alister Kunkle, and for some reason, I'm being met with resistance."

"Mr. Kunkle. Of course. You know, he is a man with quite a history." The director pulled his hand away and wiped it against his pant leg. "But before we get into that, I would like to change your impression of this facility and start over again. Welcome to Sunnyside." He handed Anna her identification tag.

"Thank you," she said, and she forced a smile. The director barely made eye contact.

"I would like to apologize for Bonnie's insistence that Mr. Kunkle not get any visitors. She was acting on a firm, long-standing directive from me." He clasped his hands together behind his back.

"She was hardly a bother." Anna reattached her identification tag and picked up her briefcase. "But I insist I complete the job I was sent here to do. Dr. Miles Griffen himself assigned me to this patient, and I would like to see him immediately."

The director shifted, peered over the thick rim of his glasses, drew close to Anna and lowered his voice to a whisper. "Before you do that, there is something I'd like to talk to you about. How about we go to my office, where we can have some privacy?"

"I don't think..." The aura of secrecy that surrounded the director and the unquestioned obedience of his secretary had an element of intrigue. "Sure, after you."

She followed the director through a narrow hallway and into a large, well-lit office. A row of tall filing cabinets in the corner of the room were like obedient soldiers standing guard. White walls and a natural wooden floor gave the room a clean feel. A large Bombay desk in the middle of the room was perfectly centered on a plush, hand woven rug. A golden nameplate with his job title occupied the otherwise empty desktop, and plaques of educational accomplishments hung on the wall. A small oscillating fan positioned atop an upside down garbage can worked the room quietly, circulating the smell of fresh paint.

The director sat at his desk, and he looked lost behind its size. Anna sat in an uncomfortably deep upholstered armchair before him and turned askew. She adjusted her skirt to make sure she was covered and crossed her legs.

"The architecture here is stunning," Anna said.

The director scanned his office. "It makes quite an impression, I know." He pursed his lips. "This facility is totally self-sufficient. Dining, a workshop, a chapel, a heating plant, a library, cisterns, a morgue and a cemetery are all on site."

Anna raised a brow. "The overhead must be tremendous."

The director smiled. "The meaning behind that statement isn't lost on me, Dr. Lee. You need not threaten me with funding. You will get the cooperation you seek."

Anna showed her agreement with a subtle nod.

"But first I would like to know if you've been given the history on Mr. Kunkle."

Anna smiled. "I assure you I've done my homework." She patted her briefcase. "Hours upon hours worth. Not to sound premature, but I'm certain he's plagued by severe delusions. It is my opinion that if I were to present him with small doses of the truth, he may respond."

"I appreciate your enthusiasm, doctor, but if it were that simple to diagnose what troubles him, I wouldn't have to forbid him from having guests."

"Forbid?" Anna slid to the edge of the seat. "How do you forbid a mental patient from having visits from doctors?"

The director removed his glasses and rubbed his eyes. Without the magnification, they were actually small and beady. "When I asked you if you had done your homework, I was specifically asking you about your knowledge surrounding the history of Mr. Kunkle. Do you know what secrets it hides?"

"With all due respect, director, I would like an explanation of what you said to me. What do you mean you forbade him from having guests?"

He scoffed.

Arrogant prick. "Is there a problem?" Anna said.

"Problem? No. Maybe a misunderstanding is all." He breathed on his glasses and polished them with a tissue. "My forbidding was put in place for the safety of my people and any unsuspecting guest that might believe his disease is treatable."

"I'm curious to know. Is he violent or dangerous?"

The director put on his glasses. "No, he's not violent. In fact, the man is as passive and gentle as a young child. But dangerous..." He interlaced his fingers behind his head and leaned back. "There are ways for someone to be a danger to others by the company they keep."

"You're contradicting yourself. How can he keep dangerous company if he isn't allowed visitors?"

"That is a very insightful question, doctor, but if you knew of his past, everything I've said would make perfect sense."

The director stared at Anna and she stared back.

"You should know that this arrangement was something Mr. Kunkle requested because he identified the need," the director said. "And it is something the board of directors and myself were happy to conform to. To this day it has proved the only effective action against the thing that plagues him."

"I don't believe what I'm hearing," Anna said. "He's being treated as if he were some sort of alien with an unknown disease."

The director rested his forearms on the desktop and leaned forward. "I suggest you listen closely and consider everything I'm going to tell you because it could save your life."

Anna sat back and immersed herself in a moment of silence. "For the record, I am appalled by the treatment this patient has received."

"He is cared for."

"I will be including this in the report due by the end of my visit, and the duration of my stay depends upon my findings."

"For the record, Dr. Lee, your report will be ignored by your superiors. They will be destroyed and false documents will be filed in their place."

Anna removed her cell phone from her pocket and placed it on the edge of his desk. "Perhaps we should test that theory, being it's for the record."

The director sat back. "No, that won't be necessary."

She put her phone away. "When was the last time Alister had any human interaction?"

The director pressed his fingertips together. "Many years."

"Years?"

"Years." His face glowed with satisfaction. "And it has kept people alive."

"You're telling me no one has spoken to him in several years?"

"That is exactly what I'm saying." He turned in his chair and looked at the diplomas hanging on the wall. "You know, I met a young doctor very much like yourself some years back. He was full of energy and looking to make a difference. I remember him sitting across from me just like you are today. He had that same hungry look as you do. He was listening to the story I'm about to tell you. And I was reluctant to give him any details, as I am with you, because I feared the words I said would be ignored. Of course, he dismissed what I said with a laugh and demanded to see Mr. Kunkle. I thought he was foolish for thinking my story was a work of fiction, and I could tell he thought I was as nutty as the patients I cared for."

Anna groaned.

"I'm sorry if my being blunt offends you, but everything I'm telling you and trying to protect you from is the truth," the director said. "An impossible truth that is true."

"I don't need protecting."

"No, and neither did he. I allowed this doctor to see Mr. Kunkle without another word of protest or caution. The next day he didn't show up for work." He shook his head. "I knew something bad had happened to him, and I knew it was because he had ignored my warning and went ahead and met with Mr. Kunkle."

Anna rolled her eyes. "This is ridiculous!"

"You can be smug if you want to be, doctor, but the man was found dead. He'd been sitting at the table inside his home eating dinner and ended up facedown in his plate of food. It is said that he died of fright."

Anna reared. "Fright? What nonsense."

The director threw his hands up. "You don't know what you're getting yourself into."

"Then why don't you give me something tangible rather than campfire tales with no substance? I want to understand why you feel it is your job to give Alister less than what he deserves."

"I can assure you Alister is cared for," the director said. "The attention he is given is special. Yes, we are limited in what we can do for him because anyone that interacts with him meets a rather swift and unfortunate end."

Anna pictured the director pulling his educational certificates out of a crackerjack box. "This doctor you say died from fright probably had a heart attack. People die from heart attacks every day."

"That man spent his day with Alister and was warned about what might happen to him."

"Like me?"

"Just like you. And it happened."

"Oh, I understand now. Why don't we lock him up and throw away the key? Certainly this man is beyond help."

"If there were only one instance of this, I could agree with what you're saying. But more than a hundred instances have occurred in which Mr. Kunkle has had direct contact with people right before they die. And to make matters worse, they die only hours after their interaction him."

The director rummaged through his desk and pulled out a baby wipe. He scrubbed his hands.

"Look," the director said, "the series of tragedies that has surrounded Mr. Kunkle is something that deserves attention, caution and action that may not be popular with everyone. I understand and accept that. But the people that died were from different walks of life. They ranged from infants to the elderly, from civilians to police officers. Whatever evil surrounds Mr. Kunkle is angry and jealous and is indisposed to compromise or mercy."

Anna could barely keep a straight face. "Well, director, that's quite the story you've told me. I'm sorry to say this sounds like the fine premise of a Hollywood movie and not the tragic life of a living, breathing human being. I've only met two people that work here so far, and there seems to be a rooted belief in this nonsense. I'd be lying if I didn't tell you it concerns me."

The director furrowed his brow. "I'm going to give you a little advice that may save your life, doctor. Go back to your hotel room, write a dummy report on your findings with Mr. Kunkle and the extraordinary care he is being given here at Sunnyside and take a few weeks off."

"I can't believe what I'm hearing."

"I'll vouch for your passionate work ethics and the spectacular care you gave your patient. You file your report and go on to your next patient knowing the decision you made saved your life."

"What you're telling me to do is not only against the law but also against my moral standings. I would also like to remind you that everything we discuss is going to be in my report."

"And I've already told you that I'm not worried about your report. No matter what you write, it will end up saying what they need it to say. Is it worth risking your life for that?"

"I somehow doubt what you say to be the truth."

The director opened the lowest file drawer with a key he kept in his pocket and removed a thick book with a cracked cover and bent spine. Ripped, yellowed pages hung out of the binding. He dropped it on the desktop and slid it toward Anna.

"What's this?" The musty stench of the pages filled her nostrils.

The director raised an intriguing brow. "That is my last chance to get through to you."

Anna glanced at the book. "This is absurd."

"Can't you put your skepticism to the side even for a moment?" The director allowed the question to hang in the air. "That book holds bits and pieces of Alister's unabridged history. It won't hurt you to have a look. Go ahead—amuse me."

Anna pulled the book close with a sigh and looked inside its cover. The pages were stiff to the touch, and several black and white photos sat freely inside the cover. She flipped through them. One photo after another showed the inside of a filthy house. Piles of garbage were stacked as high as three feet and narrow paths were routed through them. Bugs covered discarded things and maggots were in abundance. She flipped the picture over and "Kunkle/Living Room" was written with a ballpoint pen.

The next item was a letter addressed to anyone that would heed a warning. The handwritten letters were jagged and scribbled down in haste. The words spoke of death and suffering and the need to be left alone. Alister's signature finalized the correspondence.

She turned the page and a newspaper clipping fell out. She read the story of Alister's wife drowning their daughter before killing herself.

The next page consisted of several small articles that told of fallen police officers and dead civilians. All the causes of death, according to the articles' headings, were mysterious in nature but had one thing in common: Alister. They called him a cursed man.

Anna turned another page and found a neatly folded and pressed brown paper bag stuffed between two pages. She removed the bag and opened it. Written in large black letters were the poorly scribbled words, "I'll only talk to you."

"Okay, I've seen enough," Anna said, and she folded the bag. She dropped it between the pages she had pulled it from. "I won't tell you what I'm thinking because I am a professional and a lady. I want to see the patient and I want to see him now." Anna stood. "I expect all necessary resources will be in place and at my disposal without delay."

The director closed the book and put it away. "I hate to sound so glum, Dr. Lee, but if you do that, you're as good as dead. I've mourned the death of many since I've taken responsibility of Mr. Kunkle. You couldn't imagine what that can do to a man's soul."

"One more second of delay on your part will have me on the phone with my boss. I'm sure he'd love to discuss what I've found today. What do you think, two, three hours tops before they've relieved you of your duty? Make your move. What's it going to be?"

The director picked up the phone and turned away from Anna. "Bonnie, I'd like you to send Michael in. Let him know he'll be escorting Dr. Lee to see Mr. Kunkle."

The director twirled the phone chord around his finger and nodded. "Yes, I made her aware of the circumstances. But it seems as though she has made her decision, and she insists on seeing him."

CHAPTER 3

FIRST MEETING

Alister looked out the window in his room, past the steel bars and into a wilted rose garden. Two decrepit cement benches were wrapped with dead ivy, which circumscribed the garden. The surrounding grass was brown. The outlying forest had succumbed to disease; trees that remained upright were bare of bark and hadn't produced leaves in years, and fallen timber had rotted to shells. All wildlife had long ago abandoned the once lush woodland.

Two gentle taps at the door diverted his attention. Although the small window on the door had been covered with paper, he could see feet in the space underneath the door. Certainly, someone had lost their way and inadvertently chosen his door to knock on. He remained quiet and returned his gaze to the garden, believing that whoever it was would depart once they realized their error.

He heard another barrage of thumps on the door, and this time it was louder.

"Hello?"

It was the voice of a woman.

"Mr. Kunkle?"

The hinges groaned and his door swung open.

"Mr. Kunkle?"

A chill raced up his spine and he stiffened, paralyzed by the utterances that shattered the peace he had immersed himself in. Like the approach of something wicked, the hair on the back of his neck stood up, and he could feel her presence move inside the room.

"I am Dr. Lee."

Sweat seeped through his pores, and his heart pounded inside his chest without mercy. He fought his apprehension and dared to look at the doctor. She was slender and stood about five feet, seven inches tall. She had a pretty face and a kind smile and was perfectly tan.

He met the woman's eyes and wanted to say something, but it was forbidden.

"I've come to ask you some questions, Mr. Kunkle. May I have some of your time?"

Alister didn't respond. The vow he made to never speak again felt impossible to break.

"Mr. Kunkle?"

The smell of her fresh breath and perfumed body reached him. The aroma was overpowering and made his nose itch.

"I've come a long way and had to hurdle a lot of obstacles to meet with you. I plead for your cooperation."

Alister stared at his reflection in the window. What he saw was a man that was beyond help, that had long ago stopped caring about anything. His hair and beard covered his face, and deep lines surrounding his eyes told of his struggles.

He cleared his throat, licked his lips and tried to speak. A raspy croak was the only sound produced, and it hurt. His vow remained stronger than his will.

"I understand you've had to endure many tragedies in your life. I'm here to understand why people believe you are cursed."

Alister concentrated a stare on Anna that turned her eyes away. He was sure she had been given the facts and she had chosen to ignore them. He could only hope to find out why before she died.

"I am ready to hear whatever it is you have to say."

Although he knew the silence wasn't going to last forever, a tear welled in the corner of his eye for what was to come. And his vow didn't matter anymore. She spoke to him, and because of that, the death and torment would start again and he would have no peace.

"I've heard others say that," he said. His voice cracked, and his words were barely above a whisper.

Anna offered Alister a smile. "Thank you for your words," she said as she sat down.

"I don't think you understand what your words have done," Alister said. "They are enough to gain its attention, and you are as good as dead."

CHAPTER 4

SCARS OF PAIN

"I have to be honest with you, Alister. I don't believe in curses or intangible evil things that lurk in dark places and prey on unsuspecting people," Anna said.

Alister sighed. "And I see being a doctor doesn't make you any less foolish."

Alister cleared his throat and coughed. He rubbed his neck. The burning itch in his throat made it difficult and painful to speak.

Anna's focus was on Alister's palms, and his eyes followed her gaze. They were discolored with red and purple mountains of scarred flesh. He placed them in his lap, palms down.

"What happened to your hands?"

"Something terrible, but there is much to tell you before we get to that."

"Then let us begin."

"With my wife, Sharon?" he said, and his voice cracked.

"If you're uncomfortable, I can get you some water."

"I deserve no comfort, not after the things I have done." He ran taut fingers through his long, gray hair and a cluster of knots stopped his hand. "All the suffering I get, I deserve."

"I don't believe you deserve to suffer."

"Maybe you should hold your judgment until you hear my story."

Anna nodded and her hair swayed with the movement of her head.

"Sharon, my wife, was good for me, but I was no good for her."

"Because of the curse?"

"Yes." Alister crossed his arms over his chest. "But you make it sound so simple when you say it like that."

"I'm sorry."

"Sharon was the only constant in all the tragedy that surrounded me."

Anna smiled. "Did you know each other long?"

"Through grade school, junior high, and senior high. We started dating in eleventh grade and had a typical relationship of old. It was at a time when men respected women. I can remember rushing to open doors for her, and we always held hands." His eyes danced around the room, chasing memories concealed long ago. He smiled. "We would go for ice-cream sodas, enjoy the drive-in theaters and frequent sock hops."

"The age of innocence."

Those words broadened Alister's smile. "Indeed it was. Sharon wore poodle skirts with bobby socks and saddle shoes and a neck scarf with a virgin pin that she displayed proudly."

"And what about you?"

"Me? My hair was slicked back, and I always had a pack of cigarettes rolled in the sleeve of my tight undershirt." He pointed to his bare feet and ran a finger up his leg. "Penny loafers with blue jeans."

"Things sound like they were so much simpler then."

"In many ways they were, and I often wished it would never end. Sharon and I were consumed with our future. We would talk for hours about getting married, starting a family and living in a house with a white picket fence."

"That sounds romantic."

"It was all a lie. I tried to tuck away my secret of being cursed, hoping that if I ignored it, it would just go away. But soon after we married and Sharon got pregnant, complications started." Alister rubbed his chin. "She had morning sickness that lasted the entire day, and her doctor treated her for toxemia. Back then, they used water pills as a treatment, but nowadays that is known to worsen the condition. She couldn't function when she was awake and couldn't find the comfort to sleep."

"She must have been miserable."

"That's an understatement, doctor. As her pregnancy progressed, the symptoms only worsened. I took care of her as best I could, but my efforts were never enough. Everything that went wrong was my fault, and, according to Sharon, nothing was ever right."

"You fought a lot?"

Alister nodded. "It was like the curse was tormenting her and making me suffer for some reason."

"What would it have to gain by making you suffer?"

"I don't know, and that is something I still struggle with." Alister sagged into the chair. "By breaking me down emotionally, maybe it was making me more dependent on it."

Anna started to speak, but refrained.

"The day of joy came when Sharon's water broke and I rushed her to the hospital. I thought the changes in her body would make things right." A tear fell from his eye, and he wiped it away. "Sharon had a placenta previa birth, and the umbilical cord was wrapped around Rebecca's throat. The child had been deprived of oxygen and had come into the world with severe retardation."

"I'm sorry," Anna said.

"Sharon was ashamed of her."

Anna looked out the window. The steel bars blocked most of the view.

"Sharon remained silent about Rebecca's condition. As the days went by, her depression only seemed to deepen, and her patience and compassion for Rebecca had become nonexistent." Alister's posture stiffened. "She didn't care for her the way a mother normally does. Mothers are gentle and nurturing by nature, but she was distant and uncaring."

Alister repressed the swell of emotion that fought to escape. He swallowed hard and shook his head.

"What happened to Rebecca wasn't Sharon's fault; it was nature underperforming."

But deep down inside, Alister knew better. Although the curse hadn't yet become blatant in its desire to make him suffer, all the signs had been there.

"I remember this sweltering hot day when we were sitting on the patio. Sharon was in her eighth month of pregnancy, and that day more than any day before held lots of promise. She smiled when we spoke, and there weren't any rude comments whispered."

Alister chased an itch that moved up his arm, and Anna watched him.

"I brought her out a glass of ice cold lemonade and settled into a chair beside her." He smiled. "Things were perfect." He watched dandruff dance in the sunlight beaming in through the window.

"The bliss I was feeling was intoxicating." His smile broadened, and he raised a brow. "So powerful that I'd forgotten about all the bad we'd been through."

Alister paused, looked to his feet and slowly raised his focus to Anna.

"Believe me when I tell you, doctor, we'd been through a lot of bad, and for me to forget for even a moment, there must have been magic."

Anna looked to her notepad, chewed her pen, and jotted down some thoughts. Alister reached for her paper and tried to spy what it said.

"What are you writing?"

She moved away. "Just some thoughts."

"Yours or mine?"

"Both."

Alister wrinkled the skin on his forehead.

"Care to share?"

Anna shook her head. "I want to know about this day you started to tell me about."

"Good distraction, doctor." He smiled. "I wish I could have held on to that moment forever. We were friends for the first time in months, and I actually felt loved."

"That's a wonderful feeling," Anna said. "Knowing someone cares for you."

"For me in that moment, it was nothing more than a distraction, a way to help me forget about all the death that surrounded me."

Anna logged additional thoughts in her notebook.

"Our conversation quickly fell off, and Sharon broke the silence by asking what I had done."

"Did you know what she was referring to?"

"Yes, but I didn't say so." He scratched his forearm. "I didn't dare."

"What did she say?"

"That there was something unnatural surrounding me. And that it had gone after everyone I loved, and Sharon and the baby were all that I had left."

Anna placed her pen down. "Those were powerful words and a heavy accusation."

"It hit home, and it still does. My heart sank. That was the only time she ever hinted at knowing about the strange events happening around me."

Anna paused in thought, and Alister used the time to massage the front of his neck.

"And yet she didn't do anything to escape it?" Anna said.

Alister shrugged. "Maybe she knew she couldn't. She rubbed her belly and told me she could feel things weren't right, and that whatever I was hiding was making my unborn child suffer for it. She flashed me a disappointed smile and walked into the house without another word."

Anna refused to scratch an itch on her arm. "With all due respect, I'm going to be skeptical until I see proof that makes me think otherwise. I don't believe you are crazy or cursed."

"I am one or the other, doctor. There is no doubt about that."

"I believe you've been plagued by a series of tragedies that have forced you into a safe place."

"I'm not the one who is safe in here."

"It is easier to hide from a problem—"

"The people outside this room are the ones who are safe."

"—rather than face it."

"Is that what you think this is? A problem?" Alister's eyes were wide, and Anna looked away. "I think your need to find traditional answers to extraordinary circumstances has clouded your ability to see the truth no matter how close to it you actually are."

Anna turned a page in her notepad. "That very well could be. After all, I am only human."

"Well, from where I sit, it is."

She clasped her hands together and placed them on her lap.

"I see you don't like it when you are challenged."

"This isn't about me."

"I know, and I also know that you like to stay in control. That's what shrinks do." Alister threw his hands in the air. "Very well, I haven't had control in years, so it is yours to keep."

Anna took her pen and jotted something down.

"Something you may find interesting is that I like to compare the curse to a black widow spider," Alister said.

"A black widow spider?"

Alister tilted his head. "Why do you do that?"

"I'm sorry, but do what?"

He studied her. "You really don't hear yourself?"

Anna paused. "Do I have to ask what it is that I'm supposed to be hearing?"

"Your evasiveness. It's like you try and buy time by repeating my statements in question format."

"I don't mean to do that."

"I find it annoying."

"We were going to talk about why you compare the curse to the black widow spider."

Alister scratched his chin and cheek. "Well, it's death's job to take a life at specified times, and it is the black widow's job to kill the male after they mate."

"I suppose you're talking about the female eating the male after they mate?"

"That's right."

Anna rolled her eyes. "That's as far-fetched as saying human mothers kill all their young. Yeah, you will get a few females that kill their young, but that is not perceived as normal behavior. The idea people have about the black widow killing their mate is a complete misconception."

Alister's heart sank. "Human mothers do kill their young. I saw that with my own eyes." He swallowed hard. The lump in his throat was huge. "Besides, I'm merely trying to make a point."

Anna nodded in acceptance, and Alister could see her resistance. She obviously liked to base discussions on pure fact and anything else was senseless.

"Let us just say that killing their mate *is* common practice for the black widow spider, and for the sake of easy understanding, we'll say that behavior is preprogrammed by nature and must be obeyed absolutely. Suppose that spider finds one male that it likes so much it doesn't want to kill it. It goes against the rules of its programming, against the impossible, and allows the male to live so she can have him for herself." Alister fell silent and then said, "I believe that is the plan death has for me."

"Death wants you all for itself, and no one else can live?" Anna sat quiet for a moment. "So you're saying death is a person or entity rather than an event or progression of life?"

Alister swayed as he wrestled with her terminology.

"I've always viewed death as being—a living, breathing, thinking entity that kills," Alister said.

"That is an interesting way of looking at it."

"Whether interesting or not, doctor, I have since learned it is a fact."

"If this curse is living, as you suggest, does that mean it too can die?"

Alister shrugged. "I don't know the order of nature, but I believe it has feelings like you and I do. Flawed according to what our perception of what feelings are, but it has feelings nevertheless."

"What made you come to such conclusions?"

"I don't know," Alister said, and he pondered the innermost thoughts he hadn't had the opportunity to put into words. "Experience, I suppose. There are times when I can actually feel the connection we have."

"And what does that connection feel like?"

Alister crossed his legs and considered the question. His gaze moved outside the room and into the garden. The wilted roses that were trampled and starved of all love, light and care painted the perfect picture of how he felt. He felt disliked, uncared for, unwanted and alienated. The horrible feeling that consumed him seemed inescapable.

"I'm not really sure," he finally said. He found the emotional anguish he would have to endure to explain the details meaningless. The person he was sharing his demons with would be dead soon enough, so, really, how sensible would that be?

Besides, he battled those demons every day.

By himself.

"It's lonely," he said, and he closed his eyes. "So awfully cold and lonely. And the worst part is I see no end in sight."

Anna put a hand on top of Alister's. "I can help you through this."

Alister's eyes moved to Anna's hand and he pulled away. He didn't do that because her touch offended him or because it had been so long since he had had any contact with anyone; he welcomed the effort. It was just that he didn't remember someone's touch being so cold. Her hands were like ice.

"I'm sorry," Anna said. "I hope I didn't offend you."

Alister shook his head. "No, you didn't. It's not that."

"What is it?"

"Surprise, I suppose." The truth was better left unsaid sometimes.

A long moment of awkward silence thickened the air.

"I'm sorry to say there is nothing you can do for me," Alister said. "Just like there is nothing I can do for you."

"I think you underestimate my abilities, Mr. Kunkle."

Alister peered out the window. The death that surrounded his area of the building seemed to have spread. It had made its way beyond the reach of his eyes.

"And I think you underestimated the stories you heard before you came to talk with me. You should've listened to them."

Anna laughed. "I have. But I've paid more attention to the belief that I can help you through this."

"And your arrogance has cost you more than you know! Every smile, laugh and outright denial of its existence mocks it. And I can assure you that's a big mistake. I've seen what it can do."

"I'm not afraid."

"I've heard that before, and it is usually followed by begging and screams for mercy."

Anna uncrossed her legs and stood. "I'm sorry you're scared, but I need you to trust me."

Alister shook his head in irrefutable certainty. "Trust is something I can no longer give."

"I think that will come in time."

"Time is something you're running short on."

"And if I promise to return tomorrow and actually come back?" Anna raised a brow. "What then?"

Alister looked to Anna with hope on the surface, but the doubt ran deep. "Then you'd be the first to do so in nearly forty years if you want to include the twenty-five years of silence I've had to endure inside these walls."

"Twenty-five years?" Anna said.

"Twenty-five years, doctor, and stop doing that."

"Tell me, what do you think of when I say the word flower?"

Alister's expression tightened. "What?"

"A flower. Tell me what you think it resembles."

Alister mulled over her question, and no matter what angle he looked at it from, he got the same answer. "Death."

"I say it represents life, love and hope."

"That's because you're naive."

Anna grabbed her briefcase and readied herself to leave. "You never answered the question I asked before, Alister. What if I were to return?"

Alister hoped she would return in the morning, but he knew better. The overdue reminder that he was cursed would come, and the invisible demon would deliver it without flowers. He wiped his sweaty palms on his pajama leg.

"I can't answer that because I don't believe you're going to return. It's not possible." He licked his lips. "Is that answer acceptable?"

"It is honest, and I appreciate that," Anna said, and she moved toward the door. She looked over her shoulder before she exited. "It was nice meeting you, Alister. I hope I've given you some things to think about until I return in the morning. And just so you know, I will be returning."

"Doctor?" Alister asked, his focus back outside the window. "I would like to tell you it was nice talking to you, but the smile you'd give me in return will only come back to haunt me when I hear of your death."

CHAPTER 5

DOING THE IMPOSSIBLE

Alister rubbed his tired eyes and moved from the bed to his chair. Concerns for the doctor and the uncertainty of her return kept him frustrated and awake.

He stretched and yawned and looked out the window. Against the skepticism that ran so deep that it was a part of his being, he searched the darkness for something positive.

Murky shadows stretched across the garden, which was teeming with a thick fog that lingered and swirled as if it had life of its own.

Alister looked to the clock over the door and sighed. He knew every second of the three hours until morning would feel like a lifetime. Constant contemplation and a million different scenarios playing out in his mind allowed him no peace.

When he returned his gaze to the garden, a shadowy figure concealed by the backdrop of trees and morphing mist caught his attention.

He stood, pressed his forehead against the window and tried not to blink. The figure seemed to look back at him even though its features were nearly impossible to make out. A black cloak long enough to drag on the ground hung off of its shoulders like garments on a hanger.

Alister slapped the window. "What is it you want from me? Take the doctor if you wish, but leave me alone!"

The figure drifted toward him and pulled back its hood. The face was unmistakably familiar.

"Sharon?"

The pound of his heart quickened, and he became frantic in his attempt to open the window. It was of no use; it was nailed shut, and the thick iron bars outside were impassable.

When he looked back up, Sharon reached for him and crumbled into the shadows.

Anna sat up abruptly. The confusion of where she was and how she had gotten there fogged her mind and dulled her senses.

The room was dark and stuffy. An unfamiliar odor lingered about, and the sound of air blowing demanded her attention.

"Housekeeping."

Anna looked at the door, at the radiator and then at the electronic clock on the nightstand. She was in a hotel and it was half past nine.

"Shit."

She tossed the covers aside, jumped out of bed and flicked the light switch on. The glow that filled the room hurt her eyes. She rubbed away the sting.

"Come back in a half hour."

Papers were spread across the bed, and some were on the floor. Most were crumpled from rolling on top of them while she slept.

"How could I forget to set the alarm?"

She hurried around and gathered the papers, flattening them as best she could. The notes contained details of what she had learned about Alister and the complex life he had lived.

"This just gives them reason to believe I fell victim to the curse."

Anna turned on the shower; getting to Alister as fast as possible her top priority.

Anna parked her car in the dirt parking lot across the street from Sunnyside Capable Care Mental Institution. Turning off the ignition, she accessed the rearview mirror. She pouted at what she saw. Her hair was damp and flat, and a purple bag hung beneath each eye.

Pushing taut fingers through her hair, she twisted the gathered mound and secured it with a hair tie. She grabbed her briefcase off of the passenger seat and exited the vehicle with optimism about what progress the day might bring.

A few hours of question and answer would help in getting to know Alister better. There was no denying how well organized he was. He paid close attention to detail and thought things through before answering as she did. Whatever trauma infected him was hidden deep, and she would have to be extra careful in bringing it to the surface.

"Look out!" someone off to her left shouted.

A car horn blared and a paralyzing tingle coursed through Anna's body. Her survival instinct shouted for her to get out of the way, but the surprise of her situation grounded her feet. The vehicle skidding toward her seemed impossible to avoid.

The bumper tapped the briefcase Anna held and knocked it out of her hand. The driver clutched the steering wheel with white-knuckled terror, and Anna's heart hammered against the inside of her ribcage. They stared at each other.

"Are you OK?" The person that shouted the warning gave Anna's arm a gentle tug and escorted her to the sidewalk.

"I was in deep thought and not paying attention."

The man handed Anna her briefcase and waved the vehicle on. "Well, I thought the curse had caught up with you right in front of my eyes."

Anna breathed a sigh and tried to steady the tremble in her legs. "Right, the curse. I almost forgot about that."

"That might have been your first mistake." He smiled and picked up a rake.

The man wore blue jeans with a collared shirt, which looked like it had been washed a thousand times. An old, dirt-stained cap was crooked on his head. "Maintenance" in bold white letters was printed on the hat, and his first name was stitched above the front left breast pocket. He had a lazy eye that held Anna's attention.

"Terry," he said, and he pulled up his drooping pants. "I'm the groundskeeper."

"Thank you for your help, Terry."

"No offense, but we thought you were as good as dead, especially being how late you are."

Anna did all she could to hide her astonishment. It seemed as though people had no problem being blunt about their superstitions.

"We were certain you were going to be found dead in your hotel room by noon today."

Anna checked her watch. 10:23. "I'm almost sorry to disappoint everyone. But you never know—I still have an hour and a half left."

"I suppose you do. But I think you're being foolish by mocking it." He raked debris out from behind a bush and pulled it into a neat pile. "The curse is serious business, and it's quite unpredictable."

Anna couldn't help but wonder what Terry could see out of the lazy eye.

"If I'm remembering correctly," he said, "this is the first time someone made it through an entire night after speaking to Alister."

"Well, I find this belief in a curse rather ridiculous. I suppose you can understand where I'm coming from?"

"No." Terry worked his jaw up and down, and Anna saw the small pinch of tobacco between his teeth and cheek. "Not really." He spit.

"Well, now you know how I feel about the things I've been told." Anna smirked.

Terry held the rake in both hands and leaned on it. "I've been caring for this place for thirty-five years. Before Alister arrived, the land outside his room was green, and the flowers were ripe with color. But immediately after his arrival, the grass, trees and flowers died. Just like coworkers and doctors that interacted with him who didn't make it past a day."

Anna curled her lip and held it between her teeth. If she were to interview willing members of the hospital staff and gain some insight about their perception of the curse, she could use the gathered information to help Alister.

"I'm interested in learning as much as I can about the curse. Can I meet with you sometime to discuss these experiences you speak of?"

Terry looked at his cheap watch and surveyed the grounds. "I should be done around three o'clock. If you're still breathing when I get off, I could give you about an hour."

Anna offered a smile and extended a thankful hand. "I certainly appreciate your time and your willingness to meet with me. I'll meet you inside the lobby at three o'clock then."

Terry shook his head. "I think we should meet out here instead." He extended a gloved hand to converge with Anna's. "I think it best no one knows. I'm sure you understand."

Anna entered Sunnyside Capable Care, winded from climbing the steps. Her thoughts were on Terry and how he fit the mold both Bonnie and the director were from. She was certain she would find that behavior throughout the hospital. And maybe she hadn't come to counsel Alister but rather the hospital's staff.

"Good morning, Bonnie," Anna said.

Bonnie slowly stood, her eyes fixated on Anna and her face flushed. Her mouth hung open.

"I'd like to see Alister, please."

33

Bonnie remained unmoved; her eyes were transfixed by Anna.

Anna stepped forward and knocked on the desktop. "Maybe you should sit down before you fall over."

Bonnie lowered herself into the seat. She blinked hard, distance in her gaze. "Yeah, sure. I'll get Michael to take you inside."

"Thank you."

Bonnie reached for the phone. Feeling around the desktop without looking, she knocked the receiver off of the base.

Anna turned away. "This is unbelievable."

Michael entered the lobby, his pace slowed by a severe limp. His right leg was stiff at the knee and dragged behind him. He would help swing the leg forward with the use of his hand grabbing the pant leg and pulling on it.

"Whenever you are ready, doctor," Michael said. His blue scrubs were neatly pressed and not a hair on top of his head was out of place.

"I'm ready now." Anna picked up her briefcase. "Finally, someone with some logic." Although her words were spoken low, the acoustics carried in the grand lobby.

"If that was a comment about my indifference, doctor, you should know I'm not that surprised by your return."

"Michael!" Bonnie said. Her eyes were wide and her body stiff. "You shouldn't say things like that; it's provocative!"

Michael stepped to the keypad and entered his pass code. "I didn't mean anything by it." The door buzzed. He pushed it open and held it for Anna. "After you."

Beyond the door was a hub where three corridors intersected. On either side of the hallway were doors every fifteen feet, and each one had a small window for easy viewing of the patients' rooms. The white linoleum floors were buffed to a high sheen, and the bare white walls and ceiling were impossible to look at without squinting.

A good distance down the hallway, Michael paused a moment, rested his back against the wall and muted a chuckle. "I'm sorry," he said, turning away. "I can't help but picture what her face must have looked like when she saw you come through that door today."

Anna watched Michael with a growing smile. She covered her mouth and laughed. "Yeah, it was pretty funny."

He bent over and rested his hands on his knees. "I've always had a measure of doubt about the crap I've been told." He shook his head. "I can't tell you how many times I almost said something to Alister, just to test it, you know?"

Anna's laugh faded and her smile disappeared. "I couldn't imagine the things you might have been told."

Michael looked down the hallway, started to walk toward Alister's room and lowered his voice to a whisper. "When I first got here, the director had me in his office and was showing me a book with a bunch of newspaper clippings." He motioned like he dropped something. "Boom, it landed on top of the desk and a waft of dust spewed out at me."

Anna touched Michael on his shoulder. "He showed me that same book."

Michael tapped his chest. "Yeah, well, that was enough to scare me quiet."

"I imagine it would. Do you know of anyone speaking to Alister since you've been here?"

Michael shook his head. "No way. No one would dare. There is a lot of fear surrounding him."

Anna nodded her understanding. "I see that."

"He just sits there," Michael said, "day after day, staring out that window, never having a word spoken to him or a smile to brighten his day. I could only imagine what that could do to a man."

"I suppose it doesn't take a doctor to figure out that won't help him to get better."

"I'm not a superstitious person, but what if the things I was told were true?" He shuddered. "I have a wife and daughter at home. Speaking to him just isn't worth my life."

Anna clapped Michael's shoulder. "Your heart is in the right place, Michael. Now is not the time, but soon enough you will be able to speak with Alister."

Michael's thoughts seemed to drift, and his smile revealed little about where they had gone.

"He believes this curse is as real as you and I are," Anna said. "And until he begins to doubt it, I think it's best you continue to keep to yourself."

Michael opened the door to Alister's room and held it. "I understand."

"Thank you," Anna said, and she stepped inside the room.

Alister sat in a chair positioned in front of the window. Each of his hands clutched the respective armrests, and he remained perfectly still.

"Good morning," Anna said. She sat on the bed, and the springs whined. The thin mattress caved even under her minimal weight. "I've returned, just like I told you I would."

Anna popped open her briefcase, gathered her pen and pad and sat at the ready. Alister remained unmoved with his attention on something Anna couldn't see.

"It's OK," she said. "Take your time. We'll talk when you're ready."

Alister shifted, looked over his shoulder at Anna and returned his gaze outside.

"It's OK," Anna said again. She stood and went to his side. She placed a reassuring hand on his shoulder and gave it a gentle squeeze. "I am here for you."

Alister whimpered and his body trembled. Anna rubbed his back.

"Your hands are always so cold," he said, and he shrugged off her touch. "I can feel them right through my shirt."

Anna blew into her fists and backed away. "I'm sorry. This building is kept much colder than I find comfortable."

"You scare me, doctor," Alister said. Spittle strung between his lips.

Anna sat. "I won't pretend to understand why." She continued to work on warming her hands.

His jaw quivered. "Weren't you listening to the people when they told you about the death that surrounds me?"

"What they say is just stories."

"You seem reasonably intelligent, doctor. Do you really believe I'm here because of a mental disorder?"

Anna offered no response.

"I'm here by choice and necessity." Alister stared at the lumpy flesh on his palms and the dirt caked beneath his fingernails. "I came here because every tragedy you've heard about is true, every death, every fear from every person is as real as you are sitting there next to me!"

Alister panted and the foul odor of his breath backed Anna away.

"If you don't believe the things you were told," he said, "then you should go to the library and find the newspaper articles."

Tears streamed down his cheeks and disappeared into a tangle of facial hair.

"And you scare me because you are the first person to talk to me in forty years that hasn't died within a day."

"I would think that would make you happy and fill you with hope."

Alister wiped away the tears. "I can't feel the way you think I should. What I feel is the slow approach of something wicked."

"Is it possible my returning today has made your curse less real?"

Alister jumped to his feet with a snarl. "Why don't you go and tell the family members of all those people that died because of me that their death wasn't real?" He turned away, leaned against the sill and hung his head. "Tell my dead daughter that, too."

"I understand there have been awful events surrounding your life, Alister, and I'm sorry for it. But I'm afraid to say that none of it has anything to do with a curse."

Alister slapped the window. "Damn you and your logic."

"Help me help you by sharing details of your life so that I might understand what you're going through."

He gave her a long, hardened stare and sat. "It has taken me half of my life to understand the things I know about the curse, and you expect me to relay that to you just like that?" He snapped his fingers. "Impossible."

Anna started to reach for Alister but resisted the urge. There was no denying he had had a hard life, but the next few days would be the most terrible of them all. Understanding there was no curse would be as hard for him to accept as it would be for a drug addict to quit cold turkey with a pocketful of his favorite fix. Denial, anger and fear would be his biggest obstacles.

"I'm here to help you, Alister, and you should know I'm not going to leave you."

Alister twirled the hair on his chin. "I'm incapable of caring in return. The death that has surrounded me has blackened my soul and filled my heart with hate. It's a hate so consuming that I've forgotten what love is." He forced his fingers through the knots. "I don't understand why everyone is so desperate for it."

"Why do you think you feel that way?"

Alister paused and greeted her question with a smile. "If what I said isn't enough, I would like to add that I have found it is much easier to hate. Loving someone is too much work, and it doesn't pay off."

"Hating someone seems so much less rewarding to me."

His smile didn't fade. "If you say so."

"Are there specific things that you hate?"

"This life and all those who are able to love."

"I don't understand why."

"Because you are all going to die, and the only thing left behind is pain. So what's the sense in it?"

"But love is what gives life meaning."

"And death inevitably takes that all away, doesn't it?" He opened his arms wide. "This is what defines my life. The world isn't filled with ice-cream and puppies. There is a lot of pain and misery and awful things people don't like to talk about."

"Like this curse you have?"

Alister waved a dismissive hand. "I hate your questions and your being here. It causes me pain, and I wish you would leave me be."

"If this curse is real," she said, "then I'm already dead and any secret you tell me will be taken to my grave. You should relish in the opportunity to have a conversation with someone while it lasts."

"How do you not see that I have everything to lose by you being here?" He slammed his fist onto the arm of the chair. "Others won't believe the curse is real, and they will come like you have. And when they do, they will die, and that is something I will have to live with."

"I'm only trying to understand."

"I'll have to live with it, not you!" Alister turned askew, closed his eyes and leaned his head back. "What's the use?"

"Suppose these things were made up by a mind that was sick? What then?"

Alister opened one eye and focused on Anna. "I hope your life was worth this meaningless interaction we've had."

"What brought this curse into your life?"

Alister sighed, pulled himself to the edge of the seat and placed his elbows on his knees. He rubbed his eyes with the heels of his hands. "What will it take?" He heaved a sigh, ran his hands through his hair and stared at the floor. Flakes from his scalp filled the air. "That is a question that requires me to go back in time to when the curse first introduced itself to me."

Director Conroy sat at his desk; the squeak of the leather chair was background noise as he worked on his budget plan. Fingering the buttons on the calculator, he dropped his pen and sat back with a sigh.

"That doesn't look good." He pulled his glasses off and rubbed his eyes. "Not at all."

Looking at the clock, it was 10:20, and Bonnie hadn't yet informed him of the doctor's arrival. He would have bet everything he owned that she would survive the curse and begin to change the minds of those that had never experienced it themselves.

"What a mess that would be."

The telephone on his desk lit up and chirped softly. The call was coming in from the maintenance building. He let it ring once more and picked up the handset.

"Conroy."

"She arrived, but I thought the curse was going to take her right in front of the building."

Director Conroy allowed the pleasure of that thought to lift the corners of his mouth ever so slightly. "What happened?"

"She was walking to the building and not paying attention. A car missed her by mere inches."

"A shame."

"There's more. If you have a moment, I can come to your office."

The director couldn't tell whether it was the urgency or concern in Terry's voice. But in either case, his need to meet face to face hinted at serious developments.

Before he could respond, a brisk knock at his door demanded his attention.

"Hold on," he said to Terry, and covered the mouthpiece. "Come in."

Bonnie entered his office with wide eyes and a loud voice.

"She's here, and Michael is escorting her to see him."

The director held up a pointer finger and spoke into the phone. "The door is unlocked. Help yourself inside when you get here."

He hung up the phone and looked at Bonnie.

"That was Terry. He said he ran into her outside."

"Her eyes are puffy and her hair was still wet; it's obvious she just woke up," Bonnie said.

The director placed the papers that covered his desk in a neat stack.

"Her coming here," Bonnie said, "is going to make people think it's OK to talk to him."

"I was just wrestling with that thought myself."

"Just take away her access to him; let her call her boss."

"I can't." He swiveled his chair back and forth. "I don't know if the knowledge of Alister goes that high up the food chain, and I can't risk bringing any unnecessary attention to him."

"Damn it." Bonnie plopped herself into the chair that was positioned in front of his desk. "What are we going to do?"

"Allow the curse to run its course."

"But at what price?"

Bonnie's eyes focused on the director's papers and something stirred her.

"Yes," the director said, pulling Bonnie's focus to himself. "At what price?"

"What if it doesn't come? What if she's immune to it somehow?"

"That's not possible." He neatened his necktie. "I think it might be waiting for more people before it will do anything."

Bonnie chewed her fingernails, and at that moment, Terry entered the office. He was moist with sweat, and the smell of motor oil accompanied him.

"Should I come back?"

"No, have a seat," the director said as he motioned to the empty chair next to Bonnie.

"I'm not clean," Terry said, and he stood next to the desk. "I wanted to tell you that the doctor asked to meet with me to talk about Alister. I told her we needed to be discreet and that today at three o'clock would be a good time for us to get together."

After all these years working with Terry, the director still felt uncomfortable looking Terry in the eyes. Staring at the one that drifted was rude, but it was hard not to focus on. He grabbed the pen off his desktop and twirled it. "I need you to be firm with her and let her know what her coming here means to us."

"I'll make quick work of her."

The director smiled. "That's good, especially because you're leaving for vacation tomorrow. This is your only shot. Make it count."

"And you need to speak to Michael," Bonnie said.

The director stopped fidgeting with the pen. "Michael?"

"He was casual about Anna's return, and I even got the feeling he was doubting."

"I'm surprised to hear that after all he's been shown," the director said. "Let him know I would like to see him, but make no mention as to what it is about."

CHAPTER 6

DEATH

"I think I was around the age of ten or eleven," Alister said. He paced the floor, and his hands were clasped behind his back. "I was a regular boy that liked to get dirty, eat as much candy as possible and drink a bottle of pop for breakfast when my parents weren't looking."

Anna sat in a metal foldout chair, and a serious look creased the skin between her eyes. She gripped a pen in her right hand, and a pad rested on her lap. She smiled as she wrote, and Alister was encouraged.

"I had a favorite pair of torn blue jeans that I wore every day, and I always respected my elders. My parents demanded it."

Alister smiled at the memories he rarely allowed himself to visit. He made a mental note to return to them again soon.

You deserve no joy.

He snickered at the voice inside.

"I bet you were a cute kid," Anna said.

Alister felt his cheeks redden, but the thick tangle of facial hair hid any embarrassment his complexion might have shown. He always thought he was handsome but couldn't imagine how the doctor would think so from the way he appeared now. He had long ago stopped caring how he looked to others and paid no attention to his hygiene. It didn't take him long to realize that it kept people away.

"Thank you," Alister said. The complement was lost within an itch that surfaced on the top of his head. It reminded him how filthy and unappealing he really was.

"My grandmother Dotsy had been ill for weeks." He tried to ignore the desire to dig his fingernails into his scalp. "The doctors didn't give her long to live, and my mother was an emotional wreck."

"Your grandmother was your mother's mother?"

"Yes."

"The death of any parent is difficult."

"My father gave my mother as much support as he could, but he wasn't able to take off from work. The family relied on his income, which supported us week to week.

"Mother had a job to help lighten some of the burden on my father. This, of course, was the reason why I spent so much time at my grandmother's house."

"So you went there every day?" Anna said.

"Monday through Friday and sometimes Saturday if my mother was able to work overtime."

"And what would you do at your grandmother's house?"

An immediate smile took over Alister's face.

"Well, she would pick me up from school and help me with my homework. Sometimes we went to the park and even to the movies."

"How long did this go on for?"

"Several years. But one day during my senior year in high school, I was removed from class and sent to the office. When I arrived, Mother was sitting in a chair red-eyed and fidgety. She stood when she saw me."

Alister got goose bumps on his neck, which traveled down his back and arms.

"That was when my mother told me we would have to hurry, that my grandmother was very sick and in the hospital."

He rubbed his arms.

44

"Mother tried to be strong, but her voice trembled when she spoke. I never told her that."

"You were trying to protect her."

"I had to; she was in enough pain and trying to be strong for me. The last thing that she needed to hear was how much she was scaring me."

"That was a very mature thing to do at such a young age."

"I grew up fast. Circumstances made me."

Anna's stare was filled with understanding and sympathy.

"I always believed my grandmother was one of the strongest people on earth and nothing would be able to keep her down."

Alister turned away.

"I'm sorry," he said, pinching the bridge of his nose. "It's hard. My father always taught me that crying doesn't accomplish anything."

"No offense to your father," Anna said, "but that's ridiculous, and I hope you know it." She handed Alister a tissue. "Crying has the effect of balancing stress hormones in the body, and when emotions are bottled up, they can give you ulcers or even colitis."

Alister dabbed his eyes dry.

"During the ride to the hospital, my mother asked if I wanted to say good-bye to my grandmother."

"An odd question for a parent to ask their child."

Alister nodded. "As I said before, circumstances forced me to grow up fast."

"Maybe too fast."

"Mother warned me about what I was going to see, and I dismissed her concerns with the wave of my hand. I broadened my shoulders and felt strong enough to handle anything because my grandmother had always told me I could."

Alister chuckled, and Anna studied him.

"What is so funny?"

Alister tapped his temple with his pointer finger. "It's rather amusing how you think you know everything when you're so young. But as you get older, you realize how little you really know."

"I think most adults have experienced that at one time or another," Anna said. "It can be quite humbling."

"Yes, it can be." Alister looked at Anna, at the floor and back at Anna again. "As we approached my grandmother's room, the smell of the cleaning supplies mixed with the powerful odors of vomit, urine and bowel movements gagged me. The sounds of the machines working would beep, hiss and hum." Alister chuckled. "And there I thought I was on the verge of becoming a man, but all I could do was try and shield myself from the things I saw by walking behind my mother. We moved inside my grandmother's room and settled beside her bed.

"I plugged my ears with my pointer fingers and breathed through my mouth. A sudden wave of panic consumed me, and I didn't want to see my grandmother. On the way in, I'd caught a glimpse of her and couldn't get past all the tubes that stuck out of her body. They came out of her arms and disappeared underneath the sheets only to reappear with blood or urine in them. They had put a clear mask over her mouth and nose, and it would fog with each labored breath.

"When Grandma Dotsy coughed, it was deep and hacking and it sounded painful. I wanted to run from the room and find a safe place to hide. It would be a place where sickness and pain didn't exist and where I didn't have to listen to my grandmother suffering so much."

Alister swallowed hard.

"But I knew I couldn't go," he said. "I had to face my fears and say good-bye to my grandmother. And that is when I learned that by being in the same room with someone you love that is dying is to watch a part of your own self die."

"And is that the reason why you told me it is easier for you to hate than to love?"

"Only a part of the reason," Alister said. "But there is a bigger picture here. You just have to put the pieces together that I give you, and then you should fully understand."

Anna bobbed her head.

"I fought to move my trembling limbs and step out from behind my mother," Alister said. "And when I did, I no longer felt guarded from what was before me. I was exposed and truly frightened. I offered my best smile, which was quickly reduced to an expressionless slit. I tried to form a thought, but I couldn't. I just stood there and stared at her with my jaw clamped shut and tears welling in my eyes. Her skin was a ghostly pale, and her eyes were sunk in their sockets and surrounded by dark purple rings.

"'He's scared,' my grandma Dotsy said. Her voice had little strength. She reached out with a trembling hand and stroked my arm.

"'It's all right,' Grandma Dotsy said. 'The Lord will be here for me soon, if that is His will.' But I didn't believe her.

"My eyes shifted to a cross that hung over her bed." Alister shook his head and balled his fists. "My eyes then moved to a nightstand that was crowded with fresh flowers and cards of hope and prayer. I knew it all meant nothing!"

Alister let go of his tension and snickered. "Stupid people. All of them were so weak and afraid to be alone. One card in particular caught my attention, and to this day I've never forgotten it or the feeling it gave me. It was of embossed hands wrapped with rosaries and joined together in prayer. I remember thinking what nonsense that all was. How could my grandmother worry about what the Lord's will was when she was in such pain? And how could she even rationalize her suffering as the Lord's will?

"'No Grandma, I don't want you to leave me!' I begged. My mother placed an arm around my shoulder and tried to pull me close. I resisted, believing if I could hold on to my grandmother, then she wouldn't be able to go. I was angry and scared at the fact that I had no say in her death. I loved her with all my being and didn't want her to go because I knew if she did, I would be alone, and she would take a part of me that could never be replaced. Not by the healing hand of time or the distractions of everyday life.

"'I'm sorry, Alister, I've got to go,' Grandma Dotsy said. 'You may not understand why things like this have to happen. But as you grow older, you will, Alister dear. I promise you that.

"I knew she was giving up, and I began to cry. Without strain, grandmother said, 'There is no need for you to cry for me. I've lived a good life and had many joys. You are my biggest, Alister. You turned out to be such a fine young man.

"I hugged her and never wanted to let go. I stomped my foot and cried, 'I love you, Grandma Dotsy!' And suddenly, the machine next to her chirped loudly, and a high-pitched continuous beep filled the room. I looked to the monitor next to her bed, and an uninterrupted straight line streaked the screen. Then in a sudden burst, doctors and nurses charged into the room. Before I could begin to understand what was happening, I was ripped away from her and pushed out of the room with my mother."

Alister burst into tears, and Anna remained quiet and gave him time to grieve.

"The director wants to see you in his office," Bonnie said.

"Me?" Michael asked as he pointed to himself.

"You. I don't see anyone else around. Do you?"

Michael looked around and saw that they were indeed alone. "What does he want to see me for?"

Bonnie turned away and busied herself with a disorganized stack of papers on her desktop.

"How should I know?" she said. "He said he wanted to see you right away."

Michael felt his cheeks redden. He fought against the desire to say what he was thinking, knowing the words he wanted to say would only get him into trouble.

"I am going to call him and let him know you are on the way."

Bonnie picked up the phone, and Michael hobbled to the director's office.

"I should have told her off," Michael said. He stood in front of the director's closed door and raised his hand to knock. The door opened and the director looked back at him with eyes magnified by the eyeglasses he wore.

"I've been expecting you. Come on inside and have a seat."

Michael smiled. Not because he was happy to see the director but rather because of the way he made him feel. His heart pounded and butterflies in his stomach took flight.

He followed the director inside the office and sat in a chair positioned in front of his desk. He felt like a naughty school kid that had been sent to the principal's office.

"Let us start off with the truth, shall we?" the director said.

Michael nodded and felt his mouth dry.

The director sat in his chair and leaned his elbows on the desktop. "You understand that the doctor making it through the night might make some people drop their guard, don't you?"

"I do."

The director paused and studied Michael.

"And they might believe the curse isn't real because we've done such a good job of containing it."

Though the director was a small man that wasn't blessed with a deep voice, he didn't need it. He held a powerful position and used his authority in a way that made people feel obligated to obey. Maybe it was the fear of not knowing what he was like when pushed beyond a certain point.

"I don't doubt it's real," Michael said, and he wiped his sweaty palms on his pant legs. "And I'm not stupid. I have a wife and child at home that I would like to see every night."

The director sat back and revealed a smile.

"I want to be sure that you understand the threat Alister's presence poses to everyone inside this hospital."

"I do."

"I hope that is the truth," the director said. "Your safety is my top concern. I have seen what it can do and hope to never see it again."

CHAPTER 7

DEATH GETS THEM, ONE BY ONE

"You're annoying me," Alister said. He had spoken low enough that Anna didn't hear him. "I just wish you'd leave me alone." She approached him with a cup of water and a look of concern.

"Please, take a drink."

He turned away. Her care was fake, misplaced and unwanted. A surge of anger made him want to jump up, get into her face and tell her she wasn't welcome.

He looked at her and spoke up. "But there's no sense in doing that, is there?"

"What?"

Alister shook his head. He did all he could to keep the bite out of his tone. "It doesn't really matter, does it?"

"I think it does. We won't be able to move forward unless you openly communicate with me."

He wiped his eyes. "And I told you that I didn't want to talk. Doesn't that mean anything to you?"

"Things will get easier for you. I promise."

Anna held the cup out and Alister took it. He finished its entire contents in one gulp.

"I don't think you understand how painful it is for me to relive the experiences of my past," Alister said. "Your doubt—"

"I'm skeptical."

"I ask that you don't interrupt me, doctor. You wanted me to talk, and that is what I'm trying to do."

Anna shifted and crossed her legs, and Alister wiped his mouth with the back of his hand.

"What I wanted to say is that your doubt in what I know to be true only intensifies my need to disbelieve you."

"My openness about my doubt is to show you that I'm not going to hide behind my fear." Anna reached for the empty cup and Alister moved it away. "And I refuse to feed your fears."

"Your being here is destroying the peace that has taken me over twenty years to build." He stared at Anna, his breathing noticeably harder. "Even though I sit and look out this window day after day contemplating the trivial details of a life worth nothing, it is still something that is good to me." He stood, opened his arms wide and spun around. "To think that this could actually be good for someone." He dropped his hands to his sides and plopped himself into his chair. "That is something you could never hope to understand. I don't care what degree you have."

"Then help me to understand."

"It is good for me because when I'm in this room, there is no death."

"You do understand that there hasn't been any since I arrived?"

Alister pushed his fingers through the hair on his chin. "I fear that is going to change. I also believe the amount of people it takes will increase the longer it allows you to keep coming around."

"I don't understand why."

"Why can't you see?" Alister let the question linger for a moment. "Other people will doubt the curse's existence, and they will believe it is OK to talk to me."

Anna sighed. "Look, Alister, I think you've been conditioned into believing these things. But they are untruths that we need to face, and we can do it together."

Alister crushed the cup and dropped it on the floor between his feet. "Excuse me. I have to use the bathroom."

He stood, pushed himself past Anna and entered the small bathroom. An unused shower stall and a steel toilet bowl next to a steel sink left little standing room. He closed the door, gazed into the polished piece of sheet metal fastened to the wall and clenched his fists.

"Stupid bitch."

He got down on his knees, pressed his hands together in prayer and closed his eyes.

"I know you're still with me; I can feel you. She's causing me a great deal of distress, and I beg you to take her, please."

The past.

"Tell me what happened to him," Alister said to his mother. He knew it wasn't good. Nothing had been going well for him lately.

"He was in a car accident," his mother said.

"How bad was it? Is Dad hurt?"

Her body visibly trembled, and her red eyes tried to blink away tears.

"He's going to die like Grandma Dotsy did, isn't he?" he said.

She turned away. "Please, Alister, don't you say things like that."

Alister repressed his impulse to respond and allowed his feelings to be swallowed by the void forming inside him.

The elevator jerked and came to a stop. A chime sounded and the doors slid open. They stepped into the hallway and walked in silence. The smell of cleaning chemicals was overpowering, and the sounds of the sick emerged from each room and drew their attention.

When they entered the room, Alister saw his father on the bed. His body was purple, swollen and wrapped in casts. Slings and pulley systems elevated his appendages, and machines stationed at the head of the bed monitored his vital signs.

"Alister is here," his mother said to his father. Alister watched his mother take a gentle hold of his father's exposed, swollen fingers, and she rested her head next to his shoulder.

"Hang on, honey. You can beat this," she said before she broke into prayer.

Alister leaned against the wall and listened to the machine that assisted his father with each breath. This day had been better than the past few days. His breathing had become steadier, and he was trying to speak though his words were mumbled and indecipherable.

"Please, Dad, you need to come out of this," Alister said. His voice was low enough not to disturb his mother. She hadn't moved in hours and continued to pray without pause.

"Mom?" Alister asked.

She continued to pray and rocked back and forth like she was in a trance. "Mom, you need to take a break and get something to eat."

She repeated her prayer over and over.

Alister scowled. "You don't know how weak and pathetic you sound."

Her constant prayer produced nothing for his father and only seemed to weaken her.

"Mother!" His words were loud enough to gain her attention. "Stop this! You need to take care of yourself." She looked to him with bloodshot eyes.

"But I can't live without him."

She lowered her head and hid behind a curtain of hair. She swayed back and forth as she recited the Lord's Prayer.

"Your prayers did nothing to help Grandma Dotsy, so what makes you think they'll help him?"

She continued to pray, her voice growing louder.

"What you are doing means nothing," Alister said. "This belief in a godly being that might actually give a crap about us is nonsense."

Her prayer found no pause and her tone continued to grow.

"Your inability to deal with the fact that we're all alone in this world has forced you to cling to a ridiculous ideology."

Alister stared at his mother. "If you knew how pathetically weak and desperate you sound," he said as he took a step toward her, "you wouldn't be sitting there day in and day out begging for something you will never get. Stand up and find your own strength!"

In response, his mother grunted and stood. Her eyes were wide with what Alister thought was outrage, and he felt small. But he watched her and realized it had been something completely different. He stood paralyzed.

"Mom?"

Concern shoved Alister toward his mother, but before he could reach her, her body stiffened, her eyes rolled into the back of her head and she fell to the floor.

"No!"

Just then, his father's body began to convulse, and as quickly as it began, the seizure ended. He looked from his father to his mother. He was still and she was sprawled out motionless at his feet.

"Help!" he said, but the word fell flat.

And suddenly, the machine that was hooked up to his father began to beep. It was that steady, loud sound—the same one that had told him his grandmother was dead.

Alister tried to find meaning in all the death around him, but the steady *deet, deet, deet* of the machines hooked to his mother distracted him.

"These damn machines," Alister said. "They've sucked the life out of me."

His mother struggled to breathe, and the only movement she had made in the past few days was the assisted rise and fall of her chest.

"You're going to leave me like Grandma Dotsy and Dad." He folded his arms and looked to his feet. "What have I done so wrong to deserve this?"

"You haven't done anything," Bob said. "You can't think any of this is your fault." He was Alister's uncle and he had come as soon as he had gotten the news about the death of his brother-in-law and his sister's failing condition.

Bob moved next to Alister and took his sister's hand. Her skin was pale.

Alister watched him for a minute, and he could see the same weakness that resided in his mother. "What was it like?"

"What was what like?"

"When you told Grandma and Grandpa you were gay." His uncle looked at him, and Alister could see how he tried to cover his surprise. "And when they told you they refused to talk to you because the lifestyle you chose offended their God?"

Bob kissed his sister's hand and placed it down by her side. "It was hard." He brushed her cheek with the back of his hand and turned to Alister. "And it hurt."

Alister looked at his mother and wished he could trade places with her. "Before they died, did you tell them you were straight because you didn't want them taking their judgment of you to their graves?"

"Why are you asking me these things?"

"My mother and father's belief causes me frustration, and I'm not sure if I should be feeling the way I do."

"Because you want your beliefs to be your own and not have them forced on you?" Bob smiled. "I understand how you feel, but something that I learned when I was finding my way back is that a man's faith is what gives meaning and direction to his life."

"I don't need to believe in God to have meaning in my life."

"No, but your parents think you do because that is what works for them. I don't know. Maybe they feel it is a safe place for you to be so that you don't make the same mistakes they did."

"I think I understand what you mean," Alister said, his anger gone. He rocked on his heels and slipped his hands into his pockets. "Do you mind giving me a minute alone with her?"

"Of course not." Bob stepped past Alister and lightly nudged his shoulder. "You can stay at my house until your mother gets better. If you would like to do that, make sure you give Sharon a call."

"Thanks," Alister said, watching Bob exit the room. His focus moved to the machines that beeped. "And don't you guys let me down."

The machine continued its steady work, and Alister allowed a nervous smile to part his lips. He knew his mother was in desperate need of a miracle, and this was his chance to help her. He started to kneel, but something inside resisted his will.

Don't.

"I have to; it is the only option I have left."

No, it is not.

"I must."

There is another way.

"No, this is the only way."

Alister knelt and grabbed his mother's hand. He rested his forehead on her shoulder and drew a deep breath. He closed his eyes.

"Please God, help me believe and spare my mother's life. If you must, take me instead."

Alister stared at the ceiling inside the darkened guest bedroom of his uncle's house. Hours had gone by, and his mind continued to work overtime with worry, and it showed no signs of letting up. He and his uncle had said little to each other since they had left the hospital, and a feeling of dread had followed him around like a shadow on a sun-drenched day.

I told you there was another way.

A grief-stricken howl bellowed throughout the house and propelled Alister out of bed, down the stairs and through each room to locate its source.

Inside the kitchen, he found his uncle on his knees. He was pounding his fists against the floor, and his knuckles were covered in blood. The telephone was off the hook, and it beeped incessantly.

Alister hung up the phone and knelt beside his uncle. He placed a hand on his back and asked, "What is it?"

Bob turned his red, tear-soaked eyes toward Alister, and his lips quivered without making a sound. He reached for Alister and hugged him.

Will you listen now?

Alister didn't hug his uncle back. He was battling something that stirred within. It was volatile and unpredictable.

"Uncle Bob, tell me what happened!"

His uncle broke away from the hug and looked into Alister's eyes. "It's your mother. She has died. I'm sorry."

His thoughts moved fast and carried plenty of anger. "First Grandma, then my father and now Mom!" His body trembled and his throat filled with a growl that built up to a roar. "No!"

Bob paused in his grief and looked at Alister with both surprise and apprehension.

"How dare you take her from me!" Alister started to hit something but stopped himself. He stomped out of the room and headed anywhere. He balled his fists and took a jab at the wall. His fist sunk into the sheetrock, and when he withdrew it, a big chunk of the wall broke apart. He turned to his uncle. "Don't you see how much God listens and cares about the things that matter most? We're all fools for believing in such a fairytale!"

Alister started down the hallway, his anger so intense it had become impossible for him to cry. Hate was all he was capable of feeling.

"Hey!" his uncle said from within the kitchen. He came into the hallway with a face bright red with anger. "I understand you're upset and I'm sorry for what you're going through, but don't you dare blaspheme the Lord in my house."

Alister fought the compulsion to charge him and take a hold of his neck. The anger that raged within wouldn't allow him to let go and he knew it.

"What good is this God you, Grandmother, Mother and Father so passionately preach about and push on everyone when He can't answer one simple prayer?"

His uncle remained quiet. If his eyes had had a voice, they would have spat something awful in return.

"One fucking prayer," Alister said, holding his pointer finger up. "One. You go on and worship what you want, but don't be surprised if when you need Him most, He doesn't answer."

Bob gave Alister with a hardened stare that quickly turned soft. "Remember Alister, your arms aren't long enough to box with God. Maybe one day you'll realize that." He turned away. "I'll give you your space. When you calm down, we can talk about this. Right now you're understandably upset and not thinking clearly."

Alister laughed. "Things have never been so clear to me. There is nothing for us to talk about anymore. You're as confused now as you were when you were spending your nights with men."

Bob looked at Alister. "I forgive you for saying that. Now go and clear your head."

Alister exited the house and slammed the front door behind him. He wandered the streets without direction, the voice inside growing louder.

Now will you listen?

"No."

Alister sat in the corner of the room, and he tried to keep himself separated from the meaningless hugs and soft voices that told him how sorry they were for his losses. He watched the people kneel over his mother and father and bow their heads in meaningless prayers. He scrutinized the religious relics that were placed strategically around the room and above the caskets.

"Ridiculous," he said. "Go on and be herded like cattle. Your salvation awaits."

He stood and kept his eyes on the floor to avoid the painted looks of sympathy and exited the funeral home.

"OK, I am ready to listen," he said. "I want to know what you have to say."

A laugh that was distant and resonant bellowed all around him.

At last.

CHAPTER 8

ATTEMPTED SUICIDE

Alister dropped an empty bottle of Jack Daniels between his feet, and it clattered across the floor and shattered. He stumbled and fell on the edge of the bed in a sitting position.

"Completely useless—that's what you are."

He licked his lips with a pasty tongue and tried to steady the room, which spun around him. Jagged pieces of broken glass spread across the floor encouraged him to chuckle. "You're dangerous to the careless, just like me."

Though tired and numb, he couldn't escape the idea that he was alone now. It had been over a month since he had discovered his wife and daughter dead. And every moment of every day he thought about them.

"I miss you both."

His speech was slurred, and every time he closed his eyes, the reproachful gaze from Sharon forced his eyes open again.

"You'll offer me no reprieve for a couple hours of rest, will you?"

Alister stood and tried to balance himself.

"But if it is not you, it will be someone else. I see no other way to escape this."

He stumbled to his bureau and shards of glass that dug into the bottom of his feet gave him pause. The floor behind him had footprints that increasingly darkened with his blood, and a small puddle formed where he stood.

"I deserve so much worse."

He opened the top drawer and removed a gun hidden beneath his folded clothes. He collided with the walls as he made his way into the bathroom.

"You," he said to the man in the mirror, no longer recognizing the person that looked back at him. The shape of his skull was long and narrow, and his cheekbones protruded. The skin that covered his face glowed bright white and appeared to be stretched tight. The eyes sat deep in their sockets and were surrounded by deep purple rings, devoid of life and emotion.

"You monster," Alister said. He slapped his reflection. He spat on it and a long string of saliva that rolled down the mirror distorted what he saw.

A heavy breath behind him quickly turned him around, but no one was there.

Four weeks earlier, Alister had stepped around the lifeless body of a man that had tried to help him when he decided to lie in the path of his vehicle.

"I can't get the sound of your last gasp out of my mind."

His intention was suicide, but he was left unharmed, and the other man was left dead.

"Please stop," he said as he covered his ears. The sound repeated itself over and over like the lips it had come from were pressed against his ears.

"I should've stayed in the house and dealt with my sorrow alone. I didn't mean for that to happen to you."

He looked at the gun, verified it had bullets and looked back at his reflection.

"Look at what you've done."

He pulled back the hammer.

"You deserve your pain and misery, but you look to take the coward's way out."

And without contemplation, he raised the barrel of the gun and pushed it into his mouth. He pulled the trigger.

Click.

His eyes grew wide.

Click.

He whimpered and gagged on the taste of the barrel.

Click. Click. Click.

He dropped the gun and it fell into the sink.

"Damn it."

He pressed his hands on the edge of the sink and bowed his head.

"This is how my life is going to be forever, isn't it?"

He raised his eyes to the mirror.

"You're weak," he said, and he fought the desire to submit to the curse. It would be so much easier to close his eyes if the accusations stopped.

"No," he said. "I remember what you did to my grandmother, father and mother. To Sharon and Becca. You demeaned them, too, but at least you allowed them the luxury of dying."

He picked up the gun, aimed it at his reflection and fired. The gun kicked in his hands and the mirror exploded. Glass flew through the air and slashed at his skin.

Alister flinched, dropped the gun and staggered backward. He fell into the bathtub and his ears rang. Visions of Becca floating facedown in a pool of bloodstained bathwater sent him out of the tub in a panic.

He retreated to the doorway and looked at the tub. The clear image of Sharon on the floor facedown surrounded by blood and Becca floating facedown in the bathtub turned him away.

"No, you don't," he said, his alcohol-induced buzz gone. He hurried out of the room and started down the hallway.

"I'm in hell."

Halfway down the hallway, he stopped and placed his back against the wall. As he sobbed, tears streaked his face. He slid down the wall and sat.

"Five times it misfired."

He laughed to himself at first, but it soon built up to a laugh hard enough to make his stomach hurt. The idea of it being impossible to die was maddening, and it dared him to test that theory again.

"Yet the moment I aimed it away, it fired."

Once inside the bathroom, he retrieved the gun, reloaded it with six bullets and squeezed off a test round into the wall.

The gun fired, and the sound hurt his ears. The smell of gunpowder was strong and clouded the air.

He placed the gun into his mouth and squeezed the trigger three times.

Click! Click! Click!

He aimed the gun away and squeezed the trigger and the recoil kicked his hand back. He tested the last bullet in his mouth, and the hammer slammed down with a dull click.

Alister stared at himself in a jagged piece of mirror dangling loosely from the frame. His mind focused on the unpleasant smell that filled his nostrils. The ringing in his ears drowned out the sound of his tongue being sizzled by the hot barrel.

Alister pulled back the shade and peered out the kitchen window. The paperboy picked up his bicycle and got on it. He had a sack full of newspapers slung over his shoulder, and he looked at Alister's house as he rode away.

He noticed the lawn was as tall as the boy and the mailbox was so full the door was stuck open with letters hanging out.

He flicked the shade closed, and his hand hit a drinking glass off the countertop. It fell to the floor and landed safely on a two-foot pile of trash.

Alister inspected the kitchen. The sink overflowed with dirty dishes, which had migrated across the countertop, and trash on the floor was in high mounds all over the house. Bugs and critters had carved out a slick, narrow path through it.

"What have I become?"

Every cabinet door and drawer had been left open, and the contents had been dumped on the floor. Food scraps, soiled laundry and many other unidentifiable things added to the mound.

Alister turned the faucet. The pipes whined, and no water came out. He looked at the empty pantry closet and refrigerator that had been left ajar.

His stomach growled, but he ignored it. He expected the process of starving to death to be lengthy and painful.

"Good," he said, and he meant it. "I deserve nothing less."

No experience could compare with the guilt that consumed his mind and the ache that filled his heart.

The lights in the house flickered and went out.

"That's even better," he said, encased in complete darkness.

Alister sat up and found himself battling confusion.

"Something isn't right."

His body was soaked with sweat, and concern pushed him to his feet. The house was dim, but not dim enough to hide the path routed through the lanes of garbage.

He belched and tasted something sweet.

"Oh no," he said. He noticed the bulge of his belly. The hunger pains were gone.

Alister hurried to the kitchen. He slipped and fell on the slick floor before arriving at the closed pantry door. He snatched the door handle and yanked it open. Food stocked the shelves.

"You've got to be kidding me!"

He glanced over his shoulder; the refrigerator door was closed. He had no doubt it was full of food, but it would spoil without power in the house.

"Damn it."

He kicked the pile of garbage and it exploded, spraying the walls and sticking like glue.

"How many more did it get last night?"

He plopped down on a pile of trash firm enough to support his body weight. He ran taut fingers through his hair and sighed.

Three loud knocks on the front door drew his attention. Maybe death decided to come for him and it was being polite enough to announce its arrival.

"Sheriff's Department," someone said from behind the door.

Alister lowered his chin and shook his head. "And how many more will it get before this day is done?"

CHAPTER 9

A TRIP TO THE STORE

Alister rummaged through the garbage in search of something to write on. He tossed unidentifiable items over his shoulder, which landed somewhere behind him with a wet splat.

When he came across a brown paper bag, he hurried to a wall, flattened out the bag as best he could and pulled the cap off of a Magic Marker he had found moments before.

"Sheriff's Department. We need you to come to the door."

Alister pulled the marker across the paper bag and it skipped and screeched and barely left any print in its wake. He shook the marker to try to force ink into the tip and tried to write his message again. It still didn't leave any lines on the paper.

The darkness in the room added to his frustration, and the urgency made him whine, "Come on."

"Sheriff's Department. Open the door or we'll be forced to come inside."

They pounded on the door again.

Alister slammed the tip of the marker into the wall and flattened it. He raced the marker across the paper bag and it left thick black lines. He giggled with delight.

"Sheriff's Department. We are coming inside."

The sound of the front door being breached hurried the marker across the page and chased away his laugh.

"I won't give you any more bodies," Alister said between clenched teeth. "Do you hear me?"

"Alister Kunkle, are you in here?" The man that summoned him approached, and Alister retreated to a sofa in the corner of the room. He listened to the voices of several men as they advanced. Their words were jumbled and too low to decipher.

Although the sofa Alister occupied was in the darkest part of the room, the absence of light wasn't enough to conceal a thick layer of haze that drifted and swirled about.

"I only want to speak to the person that started to speak to me," Alister said.

"We just need to ask you a few questions."

"No, not we. I will only speak to you."

The officer's flashlight beams slashed the darkness and revealed many things that moved.

"I'm Sergeant—"

"I don't want to know your name," Alister said, and he meant it. "I'm sorry; it's nothing personal." He watched the bugs as they crawled and flew and wondered how he hadn't noticed them before.

Alister raised the brown paper bag over his head and stretched it flat.

The sergeant settled his light on Alister's sign and then on Alister's pale face. "Yes, I understand that you only want to talk to me. You can put it down now."

Alister squinted and turned away from the light. He had become accustomed to living in the dark.

"I can't—at least not until you understand what it means. It is important that whoever is with you understands that they are not to try and communicate with me."

"OK," the sergeant said. "You have my word. No one but I will speak to you."

"Please make sure they understand."

The sergeant centered his light on his men.

"Not a word to him. Do you understand me?"

One of the men was bent over a pile of garbage. His eyes were bright red and filled with tears and he was gagging. A rat came into view, and it continued to pick through the waste without pause.

"Yes, sergeant," the other officer said. His voice was weak and he looked pale.

"Why don't you both go outside?" the sergeant said. "I'll be out in a minute."

Alister lowered the paper bag and watched the two officers retreat. He realized the grime that stained the walls and floor had also stained his clothing and skin.

"They're gone," the sergeant said.

"Thank you."

The sergeant nodded.

"I know how bad things must look in here," Alister said.

"So you understand why I would like to go outside?"

"I do, but what have I done so wrong that you would break down my front door?"

"You stole food last night and threatened everyone inside the store. A witness followed you home."

Alister scratched his head; his skin felt no different than the mound of trash that separated him from the sergeant. "I can't remember being in any store recently."

"Does anyone else besides you live here?"

"No, not anymore."

The sergeant scanned the room with his flashlight. "How long have you been living like this?"

"Ever since my wife drowned my daughter and then killed herself."

"I'm sorry."

"Me too."

Alister stood, and the sergeant moved his hand to his weapon.

Alister paused. "I won't cause you any more trouble than I already have." He placed the paper bag on the seat. "Can we go out back so we can talk?"

"We need to go out front for safety reasons."

"It is important that you keep me away from other people." Alister looked away. "I would like to tell you about the strange things that have happened to me. It might help you understand why I live like this."

"I don't mind listening to what you have to say, but we should go out front where my partners are."

"I beg you not to make me do that."

"It's for safety reasons."

"What I have to tell you..." Alister paused and drew a deep breath. "I'm sorry, this is hard to talk about, but it has to do with what made my wife kill our child."

The sergeant sighed. "OK, we can go out back, but I'm going to have to place handcuffs on you. You do understand that what I see here makes me nervous, don't you?"

Alister stared at a pile of maggot-infested food. "Yes, I understand."

Alister turned around and placed his hands behind his back. The sergeant bound his wrists with cuffs and clapped his shoulder. "You lead the way." He held on to Alister's arm.

Alister maneuvered through the path, and the sergeant remained close. When they arrived at the back door, Alister stepped outside. He squinted against the raw sunlight and sat on the top step of the stoop.

"I haven't seen daylight in weeks." He hung his head between his knees and said, "I wish I had a free hand to shield my eyes."

The sergeant stood in front of Alister, and his shadow blocked the sun.

"I've been living like this so long that I don't notice it anymore. It's probably the most repulsive thing you've ever seen, but you should know things weren't always like this. I had a good job and hope for my future."

"There is still hope."

Alister shook his head. "The hope that I have is very different from the hope you speak of."

The sergeant stood still and without expression, but Alister could see the big question mark that hung over his head.

"I knew love," Alister said. "I even celebrated it. But now I see no worth in it. Self-preservation is overrated." Alister laughed. "I used to fear death, but now that is all I ever hope for."

"You don't need to worry anymore," the sergeant said. "We are here to get you help."

Alister knew those words came from a training manual. But he also knew that somewhere behind the badge and uniform was a man that genuinely cared for people.

"Thank you. You're a good man."

The sergeant smiled. "I know that you just need someone to talk to so you can work on whatever happened to you."

"It's not me that it happened to." Alister looked away. "Not directly anyway. I'm just an unwilling spectator."

Alister leaned so that he was out of the sergeant's shadow. He raised his chin to the sun. It felt warm and inviting, and he returned to the shade.

"I don't deserve it."

"Deserve what?"

"Anything good because of what I have done."

The sergeant's silence forced Alister to look at him. The big question mark still lingered over his head.

"I am cursed with death and anyone that communicates with me dies. That is why it is so important that you and only you speak to me."

Alister looked to his feet and flexed his toes. They were bare and dirt was caked between each toe and filled each nail bed.

"I invited this curse into my life, and it has made me endure so much tragedy that I am no longer alive inside."

The sergeant shifted on his feet. "I'm sorry about the misfortune you've had in your life."

Alister grimaced.

"I'm going to take you somewhere you can get some help," the sergeant said.

"Maybe I read you all wrong." He shook his head. "You're only appeasing me."

"I'm trying to help you."

A bird in a tree cawed and drew his attention. A big black crow looked down at him. It began to run back and forth on a tree branch and bob its head wildly.

Alister's gaze moved down the tree and swept through the yard. The grass was tall and brown, and he wondered what evil lurked in it. The trees were bare of leaves and everything around him looked dead. His gaze moved beyond his property, and everything bustled with color.

The crow cawed again, and Alister looked in time enough to watch it fall from the tree, dead. He stood and the sergeant reached for him.

"Take it easy."

Alister barely felt the touch over the tingle that shot through his entire body. "It's here with us."

"No one is here with us."

Alister sat again and turned his eyes toward the sergeant. He waited, expecting to see him fall over dead.

"You OK?"

"I'll be fine," Alister said.

"You're making me nervous."

"I don't mean to. Can you give me a pen and paper for the ride in?"

The sergeant shook his head. "Why don't we wait until we get to the hospital before we do anything else?"

"Please!" Alister said. He wiped the tears running down his cheeks on his shoulder. "I'm not going to do anything stupid. I have a few things that need to be said, and that will be my only form of communication after you leave me. I've already told you I won't speak to anyone else but you."

"Very well," the sergeant said. "I will remove the cuffs when I get you into the back of my car. You can write what you need on the way. Don't make me regret this decision."

"I won't, and thank you," Alister said, and he smiled for the first time in months. "But please, don't let the other officers talk to me."

"I won't," the sergeant said, and he escorted Alister through the tall grass and to the back seat of his patrol car.

CHAPTER 10

ANOTHER SLAUGHTER

"Please, slow down," Alister said to the sergeant, but the landscape he saw whizzing by with his peripheral vision told him that the sergeant had no intention of listening. "I have a lot to tell people, and I don't think you're giving me enough time to write it."

"I've given you plenty of time. Besides, I'm going as slow as possible."

Alister sighed and pressed the pen onto the paper. The vehicle seemed to locate every pothole, and he struggled to write. He jotted down the words as quickly as possible and tried to keep his thoughts organized. One thing he knew he needed to request was a grace period where no one would talk to him after the sergeant left. He explained that if the sergeant lived longer than twenty-four hours, then anyone could talk to him because he had somehow outwaited the curse. But if the sergeant didn't survive the full duration, he forbade anyone else to speak to him, and he should be placed in isolation.

In conclusion, Alister went into as much detail as possible about the specifics of the curse and how he thought it functioned.

Satisfied that his message was clear and legible, he signed his name and folded the pages with care. "Thank you," he said to the sergeant. "I've completed my message."

"And just in time, too," the sergeant said, and he turned the vehicle into the parking lot of a hospital.

"But please," Alister said, "take a moment to read it over before you take me inside. I want to make sure my note is perfectly clear so that someone who knows nothing about it beforehand will be fully aware of what it is they are up against."

"Why don't you just tell me what your message is?"

Alister sat motionless, dumbfounded. "It's everything I've told you, and it explains what people should do if something were to happen to you."

The sergeant smirked and looked at Alister through his rearview mirror. "And what do you think is going to happen to me?"

"I hope nothing," Alister said. He looked to his dirty bare feet. "But I'm certain you're going to die by the end of this day."

Alister watched the sergeant's facial expression change in the reflection of the rearview mirror as he read through his letter. He scowled, raised a brow, curled his lip and mouthed each word.

"Is my handwriting legible?"

"I can read it just fine. What do you expect me to do with this?" the sergeant asked as he refolded the pages. He met Alister's gaze in the mirror.

Alister held back a sigh. "I would like you to give it to the physician that's going to be caring for me."

The sergeant shook his head. "Once I get you inside, you can give it to him yourself."

Alister closed his eyes and leaned back. "What will it take?" He pulled himself close to the cage that separated them. "I can't speak to anyone else but you, or more people will die. Remember? I've explained that in the note. Wasn't I clear enough?"

The sergeant nodded. "Yeah, your letter is clear enough, but you can't expect people to believe this."

"I can and do because it is all true." He settled into the seat. "I'm sorry I got you involved in this, sergeant. But as fate would have it, you were the one sent to my house. You seem like a nice guy who cares for people, and the world doesn't have many like you."

"Thank you," the sergeant said. He looked out the window and drummed his fingers on the steering wheel. "I'll pass your note along," he said, and he returned his gaze to the mirror. "But I can't make any promises as to how other people will respond to it."

Alister looked out the window and watched a young mother pushing her baby in a stroller. He noticed the full head of blonde hair the young toddler had and thought of his precious Becca. Like that child, she was young and innocent and had nothing to do with whatever hell was on a rampage. He did not want to see that happen again.

Ever.

"The bad thing that is going to get you is my fault. If there were a way for me to get rid of it myself and change your fate, I would, but I've done everything to escape it, and nothing seems to work. I've tried locking myself away from the world so I would starve to death, but as you know by my being here with you today, that didn't work."

"I understand your concern for me," the sergeant said as he took his eyes away from the mirror. He opened his door. "But I'll be fine, and so will you."

Alister shook his head and rested his forehead against the cage that separated them. "I don't think you understand the significance of what you've learned today. This thing that follows me does not discriminate, and you can't escape it. The only thing we can do is try and contain it. And please, whatever you do, don't make it angry by mocking it because it might make you suffer."

"Why would it want to make me suffer?"

Alister stared back at the sergeant in astonishment. What was so difficult to understand?

"Because it can." Alister saw a little gray in the sergeant's hair and guessed he was somewhere in his mid thirties. "And it doesn't want you or anyone else around me. And when you doubt its existence and power, it will demonstrate for everyone what it is capable of doing." Alister sat upright and stared at the back of the sergeant's head. "It is bad to taunt a wild animal that occupies an unlocked cage. This is why I've asked no one else but you to talk to me and I've taken the necessary precautions to protect anyone that might get the urge to. People have a tendency not to believe in it until it is too late."

The sergeant eyed Alister, and a stern look crinkled the skin on his forehead.

"The look you're giving me tells me you still doubt what I've told you to be the truth. I'm only trying to save lives."

"I believe you think you are," the sergeant said, and he got out of the car. He walked to the back door and opened it for Alister. "And I will do what I can to help you relay your message. But I want to get you inside first so you can get the attention you deserve."

A surge of frustration tightened Alister's hands into fists that he wanted to pound on the cage, but he refrained. "I'm afraid I might have misjudged you."

"I've done a lot for you, and you should be thankful."

"I'm afraid what you've done isn't enough."

Alister meshed his fingers into the weaves of the metal cage and squeezed. "I will not go in there unless you pass along my note and I am guaranteed that no one but you is going to talk to me. I assure you that you will come to understand why I have to do this. I just hope you start to comprehend it before it's too late."

The sergeant rested a forearm on the hood of the car and leaned inside. "Listen, I've done everything you've asked of me, things that I normally wouldn't do because I sympathize with whatever it is you are going through. I give you my word if you come with me without trouble, I will speak to the doctors on your behalf. But if you don't, all bets are off."

Alister felt small and weak, but what he had said meant something, and it was worth the fight. One life saved this day would be a victory. "I'm sorry, but I can't."

"Not another word of protest, Mr. Kunkle. Now let's go inside and get you the help you need."

Alister shook his head. "I can hear your frustration, but I'm not going anywhere without that assurance."

The sergeant stared at Alister and sighed. "Have it your way," he said, and he slammed the door closed. He walked toward the hospital, and Alister watched him unfold the letter he'd written. He eased his grip on the cage and sat back and flexed his fingers. The metal had cut into his fingers deep enough to draw blood.

"Please, let this work."

So far he had been able to elude the full wrath of the curse, and he was confident he could keep the casualties down to a minimum if he were to remain smart and manipulate the cop for as long as he remained alive.

Alister watched the sergeant emerge from the hospital with two officers in tow. Alister figured it was the same two men that had left his house because of the things they had seen. The idea of being able to get out of this situation with only one death on his hands suddenly seemed impossible. Death would get its fill this day, and he would get another harsh reminder that the thing that plagued him was inescapable and violent.

He shivered.

He felt as though the black shadow of death had sat down next to him. He quickly moved away, and although the seats around him were unoccupied, he knew it was there. He could sense it. The hair on the back of his neck stood up and he got goose bumps.

"Leave me be," Alister said. "I can get out of this. I just need some time to think this through."

A faint laughter that was deep and sinister quickened his heart and roused his fears. He wanted to run but knew he couldn't because he was locked up with the wild animal.

"Control yourself."

He groaned, looked to the floor and flexed his toes. The thunder of his heart was in his throat and so loud he could no longer hear the laughter.

The sergeant opened Alister's door and stood with his head inside the car. "I've done all I can. I'm sorry."

"It was in here with me, but you just let it out," Alister said.

"I need you to show me the same respect I've shown you and come inside the hospital so the doctors can have a look at you."

"Please, don't do this to me." Alister rocked back and forth. His focus remained on his feet, and he continued to flex and relax his toes.

"I'm just asking you to come with me."

Alister looked at the sergeant. "I wasn't talking to you."

"Who were you talking to then?"

"Death." He licked his lips. "It is here, and I'm hoping it will show you mercy."

The sergeant looked around. "I think you'll start to feel better after we get you inside."

Alister scooted as far away from the sergeant as he could and could no longer sense death's whereabouts. "I'm going to have to decline going inside that hospital and stay here."

Alister closed his eyes and latched onto the cage. "I mean you and the other officers no disrespect." The cage sliced into his cuts, but no amount of pain would make him let go.

The sergeant directed one of the officers to the other side of the cruiser, and that officer opened the door. "I'm going to have to ask you to step out of the car, Mr. Kunkle," the other officer said.

In that instant, all of the fight left Alister and he loosened his grip on the cage. The sound of the other officer's voice hit him like an unexpected punch to the gut.

"If you don't come willingly," the officer said, "then we're going to have to use force. We don't want to have to do that."

Nausea made Alister's stomach roll. Nothing about the moment felt real, and the sounds around him had become muffled and slow. A tremble deep inside his body built and threatened to surface.

"Get your ass out of the car," the officer said, and he yanked Alister out by his arm. He pushed Alister against the car and forced his face onto the hood and one arm behind his back. "Because you are no longer cooperating, I'm going to have to place cuffs on you."

Alister's eyes bulged and his legs wobbled. His head snapped up, and he focused his gaze on the sergeant. "You!" he said, and spit flew from his mouth. "I'm holding you responsible for this man's death! I did all I could to prevent it from going after him, but you just wouldn't listen!"

The young officer cuffed Alister's other wrist and pulled him off of the car. He faced him in the direction he wanted him to walk and gave him a shove. "Keep your mouth shut. You're a crazy son of a bitch, you know that?"

Alister turned in time to see the cop stagger as if someone had landed a punch to the side of his head. He watched the shadow of death jump inside the man and make his body convulse.

Alister stumbled backward. "Did you see that?"

The young officer looked from Alister to the sergeant, confused and afraid. "My God, please help me." He wiped the blood that began to trickle from his eyes.

The sergeant ran to a middle-aged doctor walking across the parking lot.

"Please, help me."

The doctor followed the sergeant past Alister, who was on his knees crying and shouting his protest heavenward. The sergeant brought the doctor to the fallen officer lying facedown in a small pool of blood. The doctor immediately went to work on the police officer.

"What happened?"

"I don't know," the sergeant said. He looked to Alister. "He was staggering around, and he started to bleed from his eyes."

"Do you know of any medical condition he might have?"

The sergeant looked to Alister, unable to respond. He was consumed with the realization that the man that had tried to warn him wasn't so crazy after all.

"I'm sorry," he said to Alister. He fell to his knees. He felt dizzy and could hear laughter all around him. "I could've helped you stop this."

The laughter was booming and something out of his worst nightmares.

CHAPTER 11

THE MEETING

Present day.

Anna and Terry walked on the side of a dirt road that curved around the backside of the hospital. Their conversation was lighthearted and filled with long moments of silence. The meeting turned businesslike when they arrived at a small, brick structure without windows. A weather-beaten Authorized Personnel Only sign posted to the left of the entrance drew Anna's attention, and Terry pulled open a heavy steel door.

"Watch your step," Terry said.

A flight of cement steps gave way to a dimly lit passageway. Noisy compressors, the smell of oil and the trapped heat attacked her senses.

"I can understand why you said no one would bother us here."

Anna carefully maneuvered around spider webs, low hanging pipes and dipping electrical wires.

Terry looked over his shoulder. "I've used this area as my office for as long as I can remember."

The wide corridor had raw cinderblock walls and a dirt floor, which seemed to stretch on forever.

"Where does this go to?"

Terry stopped, looked to Anna and with a grin said, "The tunnel? It goes to every building in the compound."

A makeshift wall constructed of fiberboard joined together with duct tape concealed a filthy wooden desk and two chairs.

"Please sit."

"Thank you."

Anna eased herself into a lawn chair with frayed straps. Terry settled into a wooden chair that creaked underneath his weight.

"So." He leaned forward and rested his elbows on the tabletop. His lazy eye seemed to spy on the corridor while his other eye remained sharply focused on Anna.

"So," Anna said, careful not to touch the table. She placed a notepad on her lap and grabbed a pen.

"I was hoping this conversation would be off the record," Terry said.

"And I had hoped you wouldn't tell anyone about our meeting. If you did, I have a feeling that our conversation would be influenced."

"I didn't. I have too much vested here and would like to protect that."

"Good. Then we agree to keep this between us."

She put her notepad and pen away.

"Most people here would rather see you die at the hands of the curse rather than see you disturb the order that is in place."

Anna smiled. "I'm glad to know you're looking to dive right into this, and I'm not sure I know how to respond to that."

"Not all things people say actually require a response. I'm merely telling you how people feel about your being here."

Terry pushed his chair away from the table and bent down out of sight. He shuffled through something unseen.

"What about you?" Anna said.

Terry emerged with two sodas.

"What about me?"

"How do you feel about my being here?"

He popped the top on one of the cans and a cool vapor oozed from the hole. "The drink is cold, but it won't be for too long if you let it sit. Drink up."

Anna took a small sip. "Thank you."

Terry opened the other can and raised it before he took a generous gulp. "No offense, but I feel the same as the others."

"I'm sure that wasn't easy for you to say. I appreciate your honesty."

"Though I myself find it a bit curious because you should be dead. Yet here you are."

"Exercise."

Terry sat up straight. "I don't think jokes are appropriate, especially when such a sensitive matter is being discussed."

Anna stiffened. "I'm sorry. I didn't—"

"No big deal." He tried to disguise a burp behind the shield of his hand. "And I suppose I'm a bit puzzled by your skepticism. I'm sure you were given all the facts about Alister, and yet you still came. Me, I didn't hear about his arrival until after he had been here for several hours. There was this big rush to let everyone know he was here, but I suppose my being in maintenance excluded me from having very much interaction with the patients. When I had to enter their rooms to fix something, I would do so while they were outside."

Terry took another drink and put his feet on the desk. Powdery dirt fell off his shoes, and he leaned back in the chair, pushing it on its back legs.

"Regardless of the timing, I quickly learned the importance of knowing everything I could about him," he said, and he wiped his mouth with the back of his hand. "And if I would have known you were coming yesterday, I would have shared that knowledge with you in hopes of getting you to reconsider."

He drank some more.

"But I really think you should consider the things you've learned about Alister and reconsider your stance."

"Have you been successful in getting others to reconsider?" Anna said.

"I don't want to get anyone into trouble, but yes, I have many times. One thing I'm sure of is that whatever surrounds Alister is extremely dangerous, and everyone that intends to visit him needs to know that."

Anna paused and traced her chin with her pointer finger while she considered Terry's words. "What you believe surrounds Alister? Does it have a name?"

Terry crossed his arms. "That is a silly question, doctor. It's a curse, and it's not like I sat down and had a conversation with it. And I think that just because you don't believe in it doesn't mean it's not real and the fact that you've been fortunate enough not to have experienced it like many of us here have doesn't make those that have suffered from it crazy or liars."

Anna compressed her lips into a tight slit. "I believe the difficulty I'm having is grasping the idea that such a thing could be real."

Terry swung his feet off the desk, leaned forward and sneered.

"You need to understand that the answer you seek won't change no matter how many different ways you phrase your questions or how many people you try to interrogate. There is a curse that surrounds that man, and it's very real."

Terry stood and pressed his palms on the tabletop.

"And this thing you are so brazenly seeking may not have a name, but it most certainly has a purpose. It kills and does so without prejudice or delay."

Anna watched Terry sit. He was wide-eyed, and sweat soaked his forehead.

"If this conversation bothers you—"

He shook his head. "I'm completely amazed by your doubt and equally baffled as to why you're still alive."

Anna suddenly felt isolated and alone; the long dark tunnel before her and the maze of pipes behind her made her feel vulnerable.

"Before Director Conroy came here, Director Lofton ran this facility," Terry said. He wiped his brow. "The first day Alister arrived, Director Lofton had me summoned to his office. I can remember that conversation like it happened yesterday."

The past.

Director Lofton sat behind his steel desk and clicked his pen. He breathed heavily out his crooked nose, and his mouth hung open. His tongue pushed his cheek out and his thoughts were far away.

"You wanted to see me?" Terry said.

"Have a seat," Lofton said. His mouth clamped shut, and his eyes danced around the room. His pale face showed worry, and he continued to breathe heavily.

"What's wrong?"

The director dropped the pen on the desktop and yanked the top drawer open, making it squeal. He withdrew a folded piece of paper and tossed it at Terry. "Read it."

Terry sat and watched the director with tightened brows. "This isn't like you. You OK?"

The director wiped sweat from his brow and looked away. "I need you to read it."

Terry took the paper, unfolded it and read it. He tried to make sense of it, but he couldn't. "Why are you showing me this?"

"Because you need to know what it says and that every word of it is true."

Terry laughed. "You can't be serious."

"Every word of it, Terry. I mean it."

"What do I have to do with the ramblings of one of your patients?"

"That letter isn't ramblings."

"This is insane."

"It was written by a man who is cursed."

"Cursed because some of his friends and family died?"

"No," Lofton said, slapping the desktop. He sat back and ran stiff fingers through his gray hair. "It's because anyone that talks to him dies."

Terry shifted in the seat.

"I spoke to him, and my time is near," Lofton said.

Terry searched the director's face for something that might tell him this was all a joke. He couldn't find anything. "I don't understand. What's going on?"

"The police officer the letter mentioned died, and so have a dozen others along the way. He is here."

Terry's body warmed and he stood.

"I'm the only one left alive that has said anything to him."

Terry searched the empty desktop for the solution. "There's got to be some way to stop it."

The director shook his head.

"But there's got to be."

"Not that will help me."

"But–"

"Make sure no one says a word to him ever again."

Terry sunk into his chair. "This is beyond comprehension."

"You have no idea," the director said. He leaned his elbows on the desktop. "I've implemented a plan that will keep anyone from having to speak with him, and the details are written down. Make sure you pass them on to the next director and he understands them."

"How long?"

The director shrugged. "Minutes, maybe a few hours. I don't know."

Present day.

Anna took a drink from the warmed soda and fanned herself with her free hand. "I suppose I don't need to ask whether or not the director died that day."

Terry shook his head and lowered his voice. "And the memories I'd just shared with you aren't pleasant ones."

"I'm sure."

Terry spoke up. "Are you…"

"Wait," she said. "If I said something—"

"Are you capable of seeing what your coming here is doing?"

Anna remained unresponsive. The continued feeling of vulnerability and isolation kept her cautious.

"People are scared."

"I don't want to upset you, but I find their fears to be unreasonable. I came here to help a man that suffers, and I am doing just that."

"That man deserves no one's sympathy." Terry's face reddened.

"It's not sympathy; it's my job."

"What he suffers from is his own doing. There are a lot of people that hold him responsible for the death of at least a dozen people that worked here, many of whom were personal friends of mine."

Anna discretely removed her cell phone from her pocket and flipped it open. "Your finger-pointing suggests he doesn't deserve rehabilitation," she said. "I respectfully disagree." The phone had no service. The basement was like a dungeon.

Terry's stare hardened. "I find your defensive nature both misplaced and offensive. He's responsible for bringing whatever has followed him here, and it has infected all of our lives."

She put her phone away. "I won't even attempt to defend something incidental, and I don't think it's necessary for you to raise your voice at me to try and get your point across."

Terry shook his head. "I was probably expecting too much from you in hoping you'd understand Alister doesn't suffer from anything curable."

Anna closed her eyes and drew a deep breath. "Your rhetoric sounds strangely similar to Director Conroy's."

"Alister is a plague without a cure."

"I appreciate your talking with me, Terry."

"Less than an hour after I left the first director's office, he was found dead," Terry said.

"I don't need to hear any more."

"You need to know he was slumped over his desk, his face contorted with fear. Those last moments must have been terrible for him. A few days later, I discovered what he died from."

Anna started to gather her belongings. "He drowned."

Terry postured. "How could you know that?"

"Know what?"

"The way the director died," Terry said. "How could you possibly know that?"

Anna hesitated. "I didn't; it was merely a guess." She turned toward the exit.

"No," Terry said. He jumped to his feet and kicked his chair over. "I know it wasn't a guess. No one could guess such a strange death. Besides, you said it as if you were certain."

"The way I said what?"

"It was like you knew for sure. I'd like to know how that's possible when his cause of death was never released."

"I don't know what you're getting so excited about. What I said was a simple guess. And you're acting as though I was the one responsible for your friend's death."

"You dare!" Terry rounded the table, his eyes trained on Anna.

"That certainly seems to be a possibility."

"This has become pointless," Anna said as she started to walk away.

Terry latched onto her arm and pulled her close.

"You need to stay away from him before someone else gets killed."

"You're hurting me," Anna said. She tried to free herself from Terry's grasp.

"It can get worse."

"Let go of me," Anna said. Her voice echoed down the tunnel. She yanked her arm away and rubbed the sting left where he had grabbed her. "I refuse to give up on him like everyone else has because they were bullied into believing in this curse."

Terry reached for Anna again, but she pulled away.

"Keep your damn hands off of me!"

Terry smiled.

"You're crazy, you know that? You and everyone else that has mistreated that man because of some mad idea about a curse."

"How dare you!"

Terry clenched his fists and kicked the table, breaking it apart with a loud crash. He stepped forward, but the doctor was already running up the stairs. He plopped himself into the lawn chair and the straps gave a little more under his weight.

"Stupid bitch. What is it going to take to get you to understand?"

The sound of the compressors were the only thing that answered him. He rubbed his eye and let out a nervous laugh.

"What will it take?"

CHAPTER 12

ATTEMPTED MURDER

The past.

"Come with me," a nurse that stood over Alister said. "Let me help you up." He extended a hand.

"No! You shouldn't talk to him!" the sergeant said. He was on all fours and blood dripped from his mouth. "Please, don't let anyone talk to him."

The nurse helped Alister to his feet and turned his attention to the sergeant. "Please, lie down and try not to move. The doctor is coming for you."

"Oh, no," the sergeant said. He wiped his mouth with his hand, rolled over on his back and brought his knees up to his chest. "Now you're doing it." He tried to look around, but a surge of pain stiffened his body. He gasped. "When will it end?"

"You'll be all right," the nurse said to the sergeant. He took Alister by the arm. "Come inside with me."

"You've got to listen to me," the sergeant said. He wanted to stand up on something tall and tell everyone that they were in danger by talking to that man and that it wasn't safe. But he couldn't. He didn't have the strength.

"Why didn't I listen?"

Now the sergeant experienced what Alister had gone through while he tried to warn him of the curse and its dangers, and he felt helpless and alone.

"Damn it." The sergeant drew a deep breath. "Everybody listen to me!" The sound of his voice barely carried beyond his lips. A crowd that had formed looked at his friend's corpse and exclaimed their revulsion, their words a blended chorus of chatter.

"I'm a fool," the sergeant said. He could taste blood, and a chill rocked his body. He looked to the left and right. His heart raced and his eyes widened as he searched the area.

He couldn't see what he had been looking for, but it was there. He could feel it. It made his skin crawl, and he wanted to be far away from it.

He dug inside his pocket and removed the note Alister had given him. He struggled to his feet and staggered to the doctor that declared his fellow officer dead and held the note out.

"Please, take this and pass it on to whoever is going to care for the man I brought here."

The doctor reluctantly took the folded paper. "What is it?"

"It's a truth that is unbelievable, but you need to know it is a truth."

The sergeant flinched at something he saw move behind the doctor. It was dark and fast.

"Did you see that?"

"See what?"

"It's behind you!" All color rushed out of his face and his eyes were wide. He backed away and pointed.

The doctor looked. "There's nothing there. Please, you need to sit down."

"It's there," the sergeant said. He licked his lips. His mouth was dry, and his tongue tasted like metal. "Please, make sure you pass along that note. Everything it says is exactly what happened to me."

"You really need to sit."

The sergeant grabbed the doctor's hand and fixed his eyes on the doctor's in a hardened stare. "Make sure that note makes it into the right hands." The sergeant grabbed the doctor by his collar and pulled him close. "Promise me you'll do that."

"Yeah, sure," the doctor said as he resisted the sergeant's grasp. "I can do that."

The sergeant's eyes grew wide and he gasped. He staggered backward with his focus fixated on the dark figure that stood behind the doctor and flicked its blood red tongue at his neck. Its eyes glowed yellow and it sniffed and growled.

"No!"

"What is it?" the doctor asked.

The sergeant fell and pointed at what he saw. "Can't you see it? It's right behind you."

The doctor turned around and there was nothing there. He looked back to the sergeant, who was stiff with fear.

"Tell them I heard its approach and have seen its face. It is something out of a nightmare."

The dark figure laughed and rubbed its hands together. It stepped toward the sergeant, its movement slow and tormenting.

"I won't let it get me."

The sergeant drew his weapon from its holster and placed it inside his mouth and pulled the trigger.

Blam.

Ten feet before the entrance of the hospital, a loud bang followed by a chorus of screams chilled Alister and stopped his progress.

"What in the hell was that?" the nurse that escorted him asked.

Alister started to look toward the commotion but stopped himself. He knew it was the sounds of the sergeant dying and the witnesses gripped by the brutality and shock of his death.

Alister hurried toward the door. He believed if he were to get inside the hospital, he would somehow be safe from the growing wake of tragedy. But the nurse grabbed Alister by the arm.

"Hold on."

The nurse tried to sort through the confusion.

"Please, let me get inside," Alister said.

The nurse stood on his toes, bobbing and weaving as he tried to see what had happened.

"The cops that brought me here are dead," Alister said. "He warned you not to talk to me because bad things happen to anyone that does."

The nurse paid Alister no mind and looked back at the stunned crowd.

"Have you been given the note I wrote?" Alister said.

"What note?"

"The note that's going to save the lives of your colleagues after you die."

The nurse escorted Alister into a large room divided into several small rooms by curtains that hung from the ceiling to the floor.

"I need you to disrobe and put on the gown," the nurse said. He dropped a folded robe at the foot of the bed. "The doctor will be with you in a few minutes." The nurse stepped out of the examining room and pulled the curtain behind him.

"What happened to the cops outside? Did they all die? And where the hell is the note I wrote?"

The nurse looked through a break in the curtain and focused an impatient stare on Alister. "I don't know about any note, and I know as much as you do about the fate of those cops."

Alister rubbed his wrists. The handcuffs had left itchy indentations in his skin. He pulled off his pants and threw them onto the floor. "You need to find that note!"

"And what I need you to do is finish changing and wait for the doctor like I instructed. You also need to maintain your composure while you wait for the doctor. I can arrange to have those handcuffs put back on you."

"I won't do this!" Alister said. The veins in his neck bulged, and he slammed his fist down onto the examination table. "Didn't you see what happened to that man outside? People are—"

"Sir, I'm telling you for the last time," the nurse said. His tone was stern. "You need to calm down and have a seat or I will have you restrained."

"You're not listening!" Alister moved toward the nurse with a wild look in his eyes. "I told you people that talk to me end up like those cops outside."

"You were warned." The nurse shouted over his shoulder, "I need help in here!" and stepped into the room. He pointed to the examination table. "Sit down, sir."

Alister cocked his fist and the nurse lunged forward and grabbed Alister by the wrists and pulled him backward. He pushed him onto the bed and pinned him down. Numerous doctors and nurses rushed into the room and helped hold Alister down. They tied him to the bed.

Alister kicked and screamed as he tried to fight them off, but their numbers were too great. They overpowered him and stuck a needle into his arm. He shouted his protest as he watched the contents of the syringe being pushed into his veins.

The flesh on the faces of those that stood over Alister began to melt away until only bone remained. The skeletons around him shouted accusations of his conspiring against their fellow man by sending death on a mad rampage. Alister could only look on in paralyzed terror.

The door to Alister's room was opened with such force that it bounced off the wall with a bang. Alister tried to sit up but restraints wrapped around his wrists, chest, hips and ankles bound him to the bed. A bright light that hung from the ceiling stared down at him buzzing and blinking.

"Who is there?"

The last thing Alister could remember was being in the emergency room of the hospital, where he was forced down on a bed and stabbed with a needle.

"Tell me what is going on," a man that stood beyond the lit area asked.

"Who are you?"

"I ask the questions. What killed those men?"

Alister attempted to lift his head, but it felt like it weighed a hundred pounds. "Where am I, and who are you?"

The man stepped forward and into the light. He wore a white doctor's smock and had eyes filled with anger.

"I am someone who has lost a lot today." The tone of his voice betrayed his eyes. "All of the people that tried to help you are dead."

"I'm cursed. Did the sergeant pass along my note before he died?"

"There is no note."

"Please, I need something to write with. You have to untie me."

"What is this note?"

"Instructions on what you should do if things got to this point. You have to find it."

"There is no note!" The doctor's features contorted, and the veins in his forehead bulged. His face was bright red and his anger was tangible—even from across the room.

"There is a note. You need to find it so people can read it and understand it."

The doctor lunged forward and grabbed Alister by his shoulders and shook him. "I demand an explanation. What have you done?"

Alister couldn't defend himself and didn't want to. He knew he deserved whatever he got. "I've already told them, and they wouldn't listen. I see you're no different. You will come to believe that I am cursed like they did." Alister looked away. "How many have died?"

The doctor released Alister. "At least ten, maybe more. The nurse that brought you into the hospital was the last to go about an hour ago. He was completely delirious before he expired, and we weren't able to get any information from him. I need you to tell me what causes it."

"Oh, God," Alister said as he closed his eyes. "It's a vicious cycle that will keep repeating itself."

"I need you to tell me what you know."

"About the curse?" He sighed. "I don't know," Alister said, his eyes moved rapidly behind their lids. "Simple things like what we're doing now."

"What? Talking?"

"Sometimes it's even less than that."

"Tell me what I have to do to escape it!"

"I'm sorry. There's nothing."

"Why?" The doctor shoved items from a portable tray, which crashed onto the floor. The noise it made was loud and gave Alister an idea about the size of the room he occupied. He suspected the room was normally used for surgery.

"I deserve a better answer than that!" the doctor said.

Alister opened his eyes and turned his focus to the doctor. "I'm sorry. There isn't a better answer. I suggest you put your effort into keeping everyone away from me before your time runs out. Find the note, have people read it and understand it. This is the only way to stop people from dying."

The doctor reached into his coat pocket and pulled out a syringe. He pulled off the cap with his teeth and spit it out.

Alister looked away and said, "I hope that works. I really do. It would do everyone a favor."

"We can tell them you died from complications during surgery. We've already made the report about your failing health when you fell unconscious." The doctor moved toward Alister and squeezed the plunger on the syringe. A fine stream of liquid squirted into the air. "I'm sorry, but we don't know how else to handle this."

"Do it," Alister said. He turned his arm up to show the doctor a vein. "You have no idea how long I've sought death. Now I only hope you can show it to me."

The doctor settled next to Alister, grabbed his arm, found the vein Alister offered him and stabbed the needle downward. The needle broke through the skin, and when the doctor pressed down on the plunger, the needle shattered.

The doctor trembled and stared at the needle in amazement. The contents of the needle dripped off of his chin. Then suddenly, a loud crack echoed inside the room and the doctor shouted out in pain.

"What was that?" Alister said. He leaned up to try to see.

The doctor cringed from the intense pain that filled his body and paced the room. His right hand supported his left forearm, which swung limply.

"My arm is broken."

"How?"

"I don't know."

The doctor went down to one knee, his face filled with pain.

"It's here."

"What's here?" the doctor said as he stood.

"Death. You shouldn't have done that."

A second more pronounced loud crack filled the room and Alister saw the doctor's right arm above the elbow break and dangle.

"Son of a bitch!"

Another bone broke, and the doctor teetered. He crashed to the floor.

"My leg! Make it stop!"

Alister went to plug his ears with his pointer fingers, but the restraints held him in place.

Crack!

"Please, help me!"

Crack!

"I can't," Alister said as he fought against the restraints.

The doctor thrashed and swore underneath his breath.

"Please!"

Alister tilted his head so that he was able to see the door to the room.

"What's happening to me?"

Crack!

The doctor shouted and whimpered.

"Please," Alister said. "Stop screaming, or they'll hear you and come."

CHAPTER 13

A YELLOW FLOWER

Present day.

Alister pressed his hands and face against the warm glass. He closed his eyes and soaked in the heat of the day. A groan of satisfaction escaped his lips, and his shoulders slumped forward.

"I don't deserve this."

He opened his eyes and squinted. The sunlight was bright and thwarting. Browsing the sterile edge of the forest, his focus swept through the garden. Shifting left and right, he cupped his hands around his eyes, which were focused on something unbelievable.

A single flower.

There, in the center of the brown and decay, a yellow flower thrived. It was as bright as the day, and it stretched its thin, green limbs toward the sun.

"It's beautiful."

It had been so long since he had seen the bloom of a flower that he had forgotten how pretty it was. What he saw reminded him of love, and no matter how much he denied its importance, he could never forget how wonderful and intense that feeling was.

Drawing a breath deep enough to make his chest swell, he imagined the perfumed aroma filling his nostrils.

"What I would do to be able to smell that."

"You can, whenever you're ready."

Alister placed his palms on the window and slowly made a fist, imagining taking a hold of the stem and plucking it from the ground so that it was his to keep.

"I mean that, Alister."

His body shook and he turned to see Anna. "You planted that there for me. You know it won't live long."

Anna raised an eyebrow and smiled. "I didn't."

A long moment of silence passed, and Alister moved his eyes back to the flower and then to Anna's reflection in the glass. The concern she had for him was as clear as the blue sky, and it warmed him more than the sun itself.

"There is something else," Anna said.

Alister broadened his shoulders. "I am ready."

"I had a difficult time figuring out when it would be a good time to share this with you."

Anna moved to the bed and sat.

"I feel we've made tremendous strides in coming to understand that you are in control of your life—that the curse is something created by your fears."

Alister's focus settled on the flower again. "I suppose there is proof in that?"

"I remember you telling me about your uncle and how he died a few weeks after your mother passed away. I believe you said it was a broken neck."

Alister sat, gripped the armrests and rested his head. "Yes, he fell down the stairs leading to his basement."

"And what was the theory you had about that?"

"That he was pushed by something unseen to make me pay."

"I know things didn't end perfectly between the two of you. You've said on more than one occasion that you wish you hadn't thrown his sexuality into his face the night of your mother's death." Anna stood and walked toward the door. "I requested he come here to see you today so you could have that second chance."

Alister started to speak but no words came forth. The pound of his heart worked the inside of his ribcage and shortened his breath.

Anna opened the door and Bob, Alister's uncle, stepped into the room. His eyes were bright with tears. He wore a smile so big it parted his lips.

"It's not possible." Alister rose to his feet.

"Alister!" Bob wrapped Alister in a tight hug. "I've been waiting for this moment for so long." He picked him up and spun him around. "It's so good to see you."

Alister's arms dangled by his sides and something within stirred. "Put me down."

Alister was trapped within an intricate web of vivid memories from the past. It was beyond reason how that man stood in front of him.

"I want you both to get out of my room."

Bob put Alister down. "What is it?" He looked to Anna.

Alister turned away, moved toward the window and leaned against the wall. The yellow flower was now brown and shriveled. "What is going on?" He bowed his head and clamped his eyes shut, his thoughts racing.

"You said my being here would make him happy," Bob said.

Alister shook his head. "You died."

"He's confused," Anna said.

"I'm here," Bob said. "You felt my touch and are speaking to me."

"I've spoken to things that weren't really there before." Alister traced the scarring on his right palm with his left pointer finger. "I remember laying your body flat. You looked so uncomfortable the way your limbs were contorted."

"None of those memories are real," Anna said.

Alister turned toward her and gave her a hardened stare. "That's ridiculous."

Anna took hold of his hands. "You haven't been in Sunnyside for twenty years."

"I don't know that man." Alister pointed at Bob. "That's not my uncle."

"I should go," Bob said.

"No," Anna said. "You need to stay."

Bob started to leave but then stopped. He clasped his hands together and bowed his head. "OK. I'll stay then."

"I've stared at these walls, all alone, day after day, watching the paint turn yellow and flake away. I've kept myself away from the rest of the world to protect the well-being of others. I have seen the shadow of death with my own eyes."

"Alister?"

"He should go."

Anna turned Alister's head with a finger on his chin. "Calm yourself and listen to what I have to say."

Alister brushed off the sting Anna's cold touch left on his skin. He pointed at Bob. "That man died." He ran stiff fingers through his hair and rubbed his face. "Dammit, I saw him die!"

Alister went to the window and could no longer feel the warmth of the sun. It was covered by a blanket of gray clouds threatening rain. Distant thunder rumbled and seemed as far away as the truth.

"No," Anna said. "He is here, and like me, he will continue to return, and you will get better."

Alister stared at his own reflection and laughed. He saw tired eyes and hair filled with gray. "How can you say I haven't been here for twenty years?"

"You don't have to go through this alone anymore," Anna said. "I am here for you, and so is your uncle."

Alister moved to the bed and sat. He looked at the scars on his palms and displayed them for Anna to see. "Do you know how I got these?"

"No," Anna said. "You haven't told me yet."

"I do," his uncle said as he stepped forward.

Alister rubbed his eyes, and the scars felt especially puffy and sensitive.

"You were jumping a fence at the high school," his uncle said. "I don't remember who you were with, but —"

"No." Alister shook his head. "That's not how it happened."

"Well, that's what you told me."

"No, I didn't," Alister said. He lay flat and closed his eyes. "Leave me be."

"Maybe that's what your mother told me happened."

Alister's eyes blinked open and he sat up. "That isn't what—"

He looked around the room and saw he was alone. Blankets wrapped his legs, and the orange glow of the morning sun lit the room. He wiped sweat from his forehead.

The door to his room swung open, and Michael entered the room with his breakfast tray. He placed the tray down, looked at Alister, looked at the window, licked his lips and wiped his forehead with the sleeve of his shirt. He cleared his throat and said, "Are you OK?"

Alister rubbed his eyes and surveyed the room again. "It was just a dream. I'm fine."

"I thought you should know that they're going to be covering your window any minute now," Michael said.

Alister looked at the window and didn't see anything but the intense glow of the sunlight that beamed inside his room.

"I didn't want it to worry you."

"Why?"

"I'm not real sure. It's something Anna is having done." Michael hobbled to the door.

A clunk outside the window caught Alister's attention. Two men placed a board behind the steel bars and over his window, encasing the room in darkness. The sounds of drilling and hammering drew him out of bed.

"Wait! What is going on?" He faced Michael, his eyes not yet adjusted to the dark. "And why are you talking to me?"

"The doctor encouraged me to do so."

Alister bowed his head. "Why would you listen?"

Michael flipped a switch on the wall, and a recessed light fixture in the center of the ceiling glowed brightly.

"Why would you listen to her?"

"It wasn't just her choice." Michael crossed his arms and leaned against the wall. "It was something I wanted to do."

"Something you wanted to do?"

"I felt sorry for you."

"You felt sorry?"

"I see you sitting here, day after day, all alone. I thought you could use a friend, someone that openly supports your recovery."

Alister pushed the food tray to the floor. Cereal, milk and juice sprayed the wall, and the plastic bowl clattered.

Alister threw the blankets aside, jumped out of bed and ran toward Michael.

"What have you done?"

Michael extended his arms to keep Alister away.

"I'm sorry. I was doing what I thought was right."

Alister exhaled loudly, sat and rested his elbows on his knees.

"Don't you understand that decision is going to cost you your life?"

"I'm sorry if I upset you; I was only trying to be nice."

Alister ran his hands through his hair, shook his head and slapped his knees.

"That's what this is about—being nice to a delusional old man?" He huffed his displeasure. "It is going to cost you your life."

Alister leaned back in the chair and crossed his legs.

"Never again," he said, and he took his vow of silence so no one would fall victim to the curse again. He had made a terrible mistake letting the doctor get as far as she had. "A terrible mistake."

CHAPTER 14

WAITING

Alister stared at the clock on the wall. He sighed at the second hand and how slow it seemed to move. It was lunchtime and Michael was late. He is never late.

"Come on, Michael, where are you?"

He closed his eyes and leaned his head back. The tension in his neck took hold of his muscles and squeezed.

"Why did you have to go and do something so stupid? Why would you talk to me?"

He felt hot but shivered. The walls seemed like they were closing in on him, and the thought of it shortened his breath. He wanted to get away, go somewhere he didn't have to face whether or not the curse had gotten Michael. But the voice within challenged him and asked him where he would go.

"To the tree," he said. He remembered going there as a kid. He felt safe beneath the thick, low-hanging branches and cover of leaves. The scars on his hands held his attention for a long moment. The idea that the two were somehow connected backed his mind into corners too dark to explore.

The doorknob jiggled and interrupted his thoughts. He trained his eyes on the door, and time moved even more slowly. The click of the latch disengaging, the whine of the hinges as the door swung open and the appearance of an unfamiliar female nurse who carried his lunch on a tray made him gasp.

"Oh, God, no."

Years of seclusion meant nothing. The realization that the curse had waited as long and as silently as he had sent a chill coursing through his body. His sacrifice, hope and belief that Anna's message might have meaning was in vain.

"You've waited all this time and endured the silence with me just to see me suffer again, didn't you?" Alister said.

"Oh, my God," the nurse said. She dropped the tray of food and ran from the room.

"Go ahead," Alister said. He reached inside his grab bag of emotions and came out with a handful of heartache and pain. "You can have her, too. I don't care anymore."

Alister climbed into bed and pulled the covers to his chin.

"I can't fight you anymore. I'm too damn tired. You win."

CHAPTER 15

PROPOSED SOLUTION

The past.

Strapped to a bed and staring at fluorescent lights that buzzed and blinked, Alister fought against restraints that bound his wrists, ankles, torso and head.

The dizzying effects of the drugs that had been pumped into his veins had worn off, and he managed to remain quiet while the bald doctor's bones broke. The doctor had writhed in pain for what seemed like an hour, and his screams had eventually turned to whimpers. Soon after, there was silence. Alister was relieved.

A door to his room opened, and the steady approach of heels clacking against the hard floor forced Alister to halt his struggle to free himself.

"Please," he said, only able to lift his head an inch. "I beg you to keep everyone away from me; it's not safe."

"Johnny," a woman that stepped into Alister's line of sight said. She had pale skin and bright red hair. She looked down on the doctor's dead body and started to shake. "What have you done?" she asked Alister.

Three men joined the woman around the body. She fell to her knees and began to weep. She stroked the doctor's cheek and mindlessly smeared the blood that oozed from his mouth.

"Oh, Johnny, I'm so sorry," she said.

Alister blinked hard. His head swam and his vision faded in and out. In an attempt to resist the darkness that threatened to consume him, he attempted to break free again. The leather whined and the straps dug into his flesh.

The woman stood and looked at Alister with eyes as red as her hair. "You killed Johnny!" She slapped Alister's face and pulled at his clothes.

"No," he said. The slap stung and immersed him deeper into dizziness. The woman looked like a cartoon character in a funhouse mirror.

"You bastard," one of the men said. He stepped in front of the woman, puffed out his chest and held his arms away from his body. The man was so skinny that Alister would have laughed if he weren't tied down.

"I'm going to kick your ass!"

"Hold on a second." Everyone in the room stopped and looked at an older man with sad eyes. His hair was gray and his voice carried the sound of reason. "Let us not start panicking and throw away our logic. Can't you see it's impossible for him to have done anything to Johnny?"

"It's trickery, Henry," the thin man said, his chest still inflated.

"Move aside," Henry said, and he moved the thin man aside with a sweeping arm.

"We should smother the bastard," the thin man said. He was now near the back of the room standing on his toes trying to see around a quiet man swollen with muscle. "And we should kill whatever he claims follows him, too." His anger curled his lips and tightened his brows.

"Ignore him," Henry said to Alister. "He, like everyone else here, has experienced something strange that is nothing less than horrifying."

"I hate to say it's only going to get worse." Alister pushed a pasty tongue out of his mouth to try and moisten his lips. He closed his eyes and exhaled with a huff. "I'm sorry."

"Two minutes," the thin man said. He held up two fingers and showed them to Alister. "That is all I would need with him." He slapped his hands together. "Problem solved!"

Alister kept his eyes closed. "I could only wish it were that simple."

"Oh, it would be." The thin man charged Alister, but the muscleman held him back.

"Your doctor friend on the floor already tried killing me," Alister said. "I can't die."

The woman jumped into Alister's view and pointed a bent finger at him. Her hand trembled and her face was wet with tears and distorted by anger. "Don't you speak of him, you monster!"

"The needle he used shattered, and immediately afterward his bones broke one by one." Alister opened his eyes and focused them on Henry.

The woman slapped her hands over her ears. "I don't want to hear this!"

"The sound of the bones snapping and the sound of his screams were horrible," Alister said.

"Why are we listening to this?" the thin man said. He struggled to free himself from the muscleman's grasp.

"I can still hear his screams inside my head, and I don't think they will ever fade."

"Shut him up," the thin man said.

"No, you shut up," Henry said to the thin man. "We need to hear what he has to say." He gave Alister his full attention. "Why? What could cause such a thing to happen?"

"The curse."

"Ridiculous," the thin man said, laughing. He stopped trying to break free of the muscle man's grasp. He bent over and grabbed his knees. "I can't believe we're sitting here listening to this."

"I know it sounds unbelievable," Alister said. "I would beg you all to take my life and bring mercy upon this world if it could be done." Tears rolled down his face and wet the mattress. "But death is something I'll never find comfort in because it keeps me alive to see me suffer."

"What you are saying is preposterous," Henry said.

"I don't blame you for disbelieving the things I am saying," Alister said. He looked at Henry out of the corner of his eye. "I would think you were crazy, too. But you need to know that I am an incurable disease that will infect anyone that comes near."

"Why do we continue to listen to this nut?" the thin man said.

"He has a point," Alister said. "I need to be locked away somewhere where no one will ever find me or think to look. It needs to be a place I could never hope to escape."

Henry stood, paced and rubbed his chin in a long moment of quiet contemplation. "You do realize what you are asking us to do?"

"I do." Alister paused to search for any hesitation within and couldn't find any. "I'm smart enough to know that is the only way."

"And you're certain about this?"

"Why don't we give him a lollypop on the way out?" the thin man said.

"Quiet," Henry said. "We need to consider what he is saying. We don't have a logical explanation to rationalize what is happening here."

"By my count," Alister said, "there is only one person in this room that hasn't said anything to me. And that means that there will be only one left standing at the end of this day."

"Who?" Henry said, pointing at the muscleman. "Milos?"

Alister did not look at him. "If that is his name, yes. And if he was smart, he'd leave it like that."

The thin man looked to Milos. "You see that? You're the lucky one."

Milos smiled and relaxed.

"Well," the thin man said. "If I'm going to die, I might as well take him with me." He sprang forward and before Milos and Henry could react, he was on top of Alister. His hands were wrapped around his unprotected throat and he squeezed as hard as he could.

"Die, you son of a bitch!"

Alister's lips flapped, thick saliva flew from his mouth and he struggled to breathe. Blackness started to fill his vision, and he no longer wanted to resist it, believing that if he could reach its source, he wouldn't have to come back.

Henry and Milos reached the thin man and tried to pull him off of Alister.

The woman jumped up and down. "Kill the bastard," she said. "Choke the life out of him!"

The thin man stiffened and gasped. Milos and Henry released him and backed away.

"Get it off of me," the thin man said. He grabbed at his throat and wrestled with something unseen. His eyes grew wide and bulged.

The woman instantly quieted and backed away.

The thin man reached for Henry, but Henry pulled away as if the man were diseased and contagious.

The thin man fell to the floor and continued his struggle with something unseen. He gasped, choked, convulsed, and moments after it began, it ended. The marks of handprints outlined by a formed bruise created instant panic in the room.

"I told you," Alister said. "Now stop wasting time and get me where it won't have the chance to do this ever again."

CHAPTER 16

UNEXPECTED VISIT

Present day.

"Sit," Bonnie said to her seventy-pound golden retriever General.

General calmed down and sat. He drew his ears back, wagged his tail and whined.

Bonnie laughed. "You're such a faker."

General licked her hand.

"You're a good boy." She scratched his head and attached a chain to his collar. "Maybe I can take you to work so you can bite that creepy doctor right on her ass."

General barked.

"Yeah, I know. She probably tastes bad," she said as she patted his back. "Come on."

General charged toward the door and pulled Bonnie along. She yanked back on his chain, but he didn't slow until he reached the door.

"Don't pull on me when we get outside. The ground is wet, and you'll make me fall."

Bonnie pulled the hood of her raincoat over her head and slipped her feet into rubber boots.

"Let's make this quick," she said. "I want to be back inside before the downpour starts up again."

She opened the door and General pulled her down the steps. He pulled Bonnie across the driveway and stopped at his favorite tree.

Bonnie slipped in the mud and sighed at a sudden downpour. "So much for beating the rain, General."

She squinted and turned away from the driving rain that pelted her face.

"Just what I want running around the house—a wet dog."

General didn't seem to notice the rain. He sniffed the base of the tree and became fixated on one spot. He lifted a leg and peed.

"You're crazy," Bonnie said. She tugged on General's leash. "Just like Michael." She shook her head. "He's denying the curse and yet I've seen what it can do! People have died," she said. "A lot of good people."

Never in her twenty-plus years of service at Sunnyside had anyone make it through the night after communicating with Alister. And after years of no activity surrounding Alister, this doctor comes out of nowhere and not only lives through the night after seeing Alister, but she also puts the curse's existence in question.

"Something bad is coming," she said, and a shiver rocked her body. "I can feel it."

A motion-activated light blinked on around the backside of the house. She tightened her grip on General's leash and watched the illuminated area. General growled and the hair on the nape of his neck stood up.

"Quiet," Bonnie said as she tugged on his leash.

General continued to growl. His eyes were fixated on the light and his tail was pointed straight behind him.

"Come on, General. Let's get inside."

Bonnie walked toward the house but could only go as far as the length of the chain. General remained unmoved, his stare transfixed and his growl deep.

"General," she said as she tugged on his leash. "Come."

General took off. His sudden burst of speed caught Bonnie off guard. Her head snapped back and her shoulders were ripped forward. She slipped in the mud and fell face down in a puddle. She looked up to see General disappear around the back of the house.

Bonnie struggled to her feet and wiped the mud from her eyes. She took a step toward the light, and General yipped.

"General?"

The rain stopped and the light flicked off. The yard was filled with darkness, and ominous shadows backed her up and encouraged her to run to the front door and into the house. She slammed the door behind her and locked the deadbolt.

She pressed her back against the door and panted. The beat of her heart was so intense it made her limbs tremble. "What in the hell was that?"

"You should learn to mind your own business."

Bonnie's eyes went wide and focused on the silhouette of a person that walked toward her.

"I want to know what you are doing in my house."

"But this is my house," Bonnie said, and she reached for the doorknob. She twisted the handle and pulled on the door.

The deadbolt held.

"I think you're mistaken," the shrouded person said. "This is my house and I want you out!"

CHAPTER 17

POWER OF IMAGINATION

"Breakfast is served."

Alister sat up and searched the darkened room. A blurry shadow moved about and the confusion of his sudden awakening made it hard to understand what was happening.

"It is a beautiful day, and you are sleeping it away."

Alister swung his feet off the bed and placed them on the floor. He picked the sleep out of the corners of his eyes. Nothing about the moment seemed real.

"The sun is shining, and there isn't a cloud in the sky."

"It's still dark," Alister said, his voice raspy.

"Only in this room. I can only hope you will find a way to get yourself outside."

Alister rubbed his face, fingered his beard and groaned.

"The air is cool, and the smell of fires burning certainly makes the statement that fall has arrived."

The light in the room blinked on and Alister clamped his eyes shut.

"I've made it through an entire day."

Alister forced his eyes open in time to see Michael sitting on the bed beside him. He shifted his weight.

"You know what that means, and you should be happy," Michael said.

"I am."

Alister looked at the covered window and then at the clock above the door. Nine o'clock.

"How long was I sleeping for?"

"Since yesterday afternoon." Michael motioned toward the food tray he had placed on the table. "I'm sure you're hungry."

Alister gave him a courteous look. Pancakes, orange juice and two slices of burnt bread were on the tray.

"Confused is more like it."

"You just need a little time to wake up."

Alister sat in silence for a moment. "I don't understand how you are here." He stood, went into the bathroom and closed the door, leaving it open a crack. "When you didn't return after talking to me yesterday, I thought for sure the curse had gotten you."

"I told Dr. Lee how upset you were when I spoke to you. She thought it best I keep away from you for the rest of the day."

Alister flushed the toilet and came out of the bathroom. "What? Why? She had to know my worry of the curse returning would have mc up all night."

Michael looked to the clock and smiled. "She said my returning this morning would have a much bigger impact on you, that it would prove that there was no such a thing as a curse."

"Is that what she said?"

Michael shook his head. "I can't help but think that maybe there never was a curse to begin with."

"If that were true, then how do you explain everything that has happened?"

Michael shrugged.

"What about all those people that died?"

He shrugged again. "Have you considered the possibility that your mind might be playing tricks on you?"

Alister shook his head. "If it were my mind that was playing the tricks, then how would you know everything you know?"

"I don't know...I'm just saying. Maybe some of the things you believe happened never really did."

Alister scratched his head and pursed his lips while he considered Michael's words.

"If it were my mind playing tricks," Alister asked, "wouldn't it only be inside my head? And how would you know about it?"

"Who knows?" Michael asked with a smile. "Maybe I'm not really real but only a thing alive inside your imagination."

"No," Alister said. "My experiences tell me something else."

Michael stood. "The doctor has been here for a few hours. She's been waiting for you to wake up. There's something she's been wanting to show you."

Michael walked to the door and Alister got back into bed.

"Tell her I'm not interested, that she should leave me alone." He pulled the blanket up to his chin and turned to his side. "You both should or other people might think it's OK to talk to me."

"Not this again."

Alister allowed a smile to take over his face. His back was to Michael.

"The doctor told me you might say something like that. She wanted me to tell you that you've already broken your vow of silence to two people and nothing has happened to either one of them."

Michael exited the room and Alister rolled onto his back. He sighed, interlaced his fingers and rested his hands on his chest. In this moment, it was as though someone had lifted a thousand pounds off of his shoulders.

Although the idea of the curse being created by an overactive imagination sounded ridiculous to Alister, the possibility that the curse was ending was becoming more real. If he was going to be honest with himself, it felt good.

"Damn good."

CHAPTER 18

SMALL ROOM

The past.

"Hello?"

Alister listened to the echo of his voice quickly fade. The room was musty, unquestionably made of concrete and no bigger than eight by eight square feet. He stood and reached his hand up to touch the ceiling. Debris rained down around him and he tasted dust.

"Can anyone hear me?"

When he awoke, he was stiff from the odd way he had been lying on the hard floor, and the absence of light played tricks on his mind. He would see things that made him curious.

He moved around with caution. His hands were extended out in front of him in search of anything solid, and after taking a few baby steps forward, his fingertips swiped the rough surface of the wall. He felt for detail and easily discerned brick and mortar. On the wall, a slight protrusion with a uniform vertical crack went from the floor to the ceiling, cut across horizontally for about three feet and dropped back down to the floor. That portion of the wall was colder than the brick and perfectly flat.

"It has to be a steel door."

The handle had been removed, and Alister assumed it had been sealed from the outside. It was obvious Henry, the red-headed woman that looked like a cartoon character and the quiet guy bulging with muscle must have listened to his instructions and locked him away.

"Finally."

He moved to what he thought was the center of the room and sat. Something hard poked him, and he searched for the object.

A thin metal item about five inches long and weighing a couple of ounces intrigued him. He ran his fingers up and down the shaft for any clue as to what he had found. It had a cylindrical shape throughout and held the chill of the room. A small button stuck out and he pressed it.

Click.

The object shifted in his hand ever so slightly, and he ran his fingers over it again to try and identify any change.

"Ouch."

It sliced his skin and he pulled away. A switchblade. He understood the people that had locked him in the room had left it for him to use.

CHAPTER 19

GIVING IN

Present day.

"Hello, doctor," Alister said. He watched Anna enter his room and close the door. She set her briefcase down and looked at him curiously.

"What's this?"

"A new leaf." He looked at his hands. They were shaking. "I've had some time to think, and I wanted to tell you how glad I am that you didn't give up on me after yesterday." He looked at her. "I wanted to thank you for that."

Anna smiled and so did Alister.

"I think I'm finally starting to understand," he said. "You have nerve to stand up to the curse. You were told about all the bad things that happen to people and what might happen to you, but you continue to come. The possibility of endangering yourself for my well-being has meant nothing to you." He licked his lips. "Selfless. And when you told me you were going to return the next day, you did. You didn't take the easy way out, and I realize it's because you care."

Anna placed a hand on the back of Alister's chair and leaned against it, her focus so intense it penetrated into his soul. "I'm happy for you, Alister. I really am. Today is a new beginning for you."

"Something inside is tired of resisting the idea of getting better, and I think it's time I take down the barrier."

Anna's smile stretched wide enough to show her teeth. "I see something special inside you that's been struggling to get out."

Alister looked at the window and a knot in the center of the plywood that covered his window held his attention.

"I won't allow that part of you to rot inside this hospital," Anna said. Her eyes were glassy and her voice was filled with just enough passion to draw Alister's eyes away from the swirl of the wood.

"Michael had mentioned that there was something you wanted to show me?"

"There is."

"I'm nervous, and I'm trying desperately to hide it."

Anna smiled. "And I'm nervous for you, but I need you to trust me."

"I do," Alister said. "I want you to know that I really was hoping you were going to come back after the first day I met you, but something inside wouldn't allow me to believe you would. I decided that night as I lay in bed unable to sleep that I would rather find out I was crazy rather than a man cursed."

Anna slipped her hands into her pockets, withdrew them and folded her arms across her chest.

"I can't explain how relieved I was when you walked through that door the next day," Alister said. He laughed, shook his head and sat. "I was happy with the idea I might be crazy and my past was nothing more than a fantasy."

"It is only natural for what you're going through to have a variety of emotions—some completely opposite from others and even conflicting feelings within the same emotion."

Alister stood, turned away and clenched his fists.

"Alister?"

He relaxed his hands and tapped his temple. "Something isn't right. Your kindness, even in moments such as this, can force my anger."

"We will learn to control that."

"I suppose a step in the healing process starts with facing whatever awaits me outside?"

"It is."

"And you won't tell me what that is?"

"To tell you just wouldn't do. You've got to leave this room and see what it is with your own eyes so you believe."

Alister sat on the bed and looked around his small room. "You want me to leave here?"

Anna nodded. "But only for as long as you're comfortable."

Alister felt the rumble of sudden uneasiness roar inside his gut and squash his bravery. "But I haven't stepped foot outside this room in twenty years."

"Do you trust me?"

"Enough that I'm talking to you when my rational mind tells me not to."

"Then confront your fears and come outside with me."

Alister wanted to protest, but he was serious when he said he didn't want to run from his fears any longer.

"I assure you there is something great waiting for you outside this room—something that will change your outlook."

"On what?"

"That's the reward."

Alister longed to accept Anna's invitation, but his obedience settled in his feet, and they were too heavy to lift.

"I don't think I can do this," he said.

"And I believe you can."

He wanted to stand and walk to the door, but his legs shook so hard he didn't believe he would be able to maintain his balance. He felt like a frightened little boy hiding beneath his covers and trembling at the strange sounds that came from his closet.

"I can't." The words were hard to say.

Anna knelt in front of Alister and took his hand. "In this moment, your decision to resist your hesitation could bring you one step closer to finding an answer to the questions that plague you. You could gain the freedom from this curse you have been so desperate to achieve."

Alister wiped the sweat from his scar-ravaged palms on his pant leg. He drew a deep breath and stood. "OK, I'm going to do this."

Anna stood with him.

"But I want to be sure no one else is going to try and speak to me."

"I've already made such arrangements." Anna moved to Alister's closet. "No one will be present where we are going."

"OK," he said. He could no longer ignore the rubbery feeling in his legs and sat. "I just need a minute."

"Take as much time as you need." She took a light jacket out of the closet. "You need to put this on; there is a chill in the air that'll go right through you."

She dropped the coat at the foot of the bed, and a musty gust of air rushed up to Alister's nostrils.

"Once you're ready, call for me," she said. "I'll be right outside your door."

The past.

Alister held a knife in both hands, and his arms were raised over his head. The blade was aimed at his stomach. Sweat soaked his face and he struggled against two different desires.

He wanted to pull the knife downward, push it into his belly and twist it around until his innards spilled onto the floor and his life drained away. The other part begged him to put the knife down and forget that the blade would do enough damage to kill.

"Either way, what does it really matter?"

The room was empty and small, and the echo of his voice was dull.

"These struggles mean nothing."

Alister growled and pulled the knife downward with all of his strength.

"I do this—"

Something unseen held his hands still.

"—for the well-being of others."

He strained against the invisible force but was unable to move an inch. Tired, the fight went out of his arms, and he lowered his hands to his lap.

"Just as I thought—a stupid idea."

He threw the knife, and it bounced off the wall and clattered on the ground. It landed somewhere near him.

"Something tells me you're not done with me yet."

Alister lay prone. The cement floor was cold and hard, and the air had the smell of something old.

"I can only imagine how this one is going to end."

A chill rocked his body. He curled himself into the fetal position and closed his eyes.

CHAPTER 20

DISCOVERING MORTALITY

Present day.

"I can't do it," Alister said. The indecision that swirled within made him so uncomfortable that he wanted out of his own skin. "I just can't go outside."

He pressed his back against the wall and slid down until he sat.

"I just can't."

He wrapped his arms around his legs and squeezed them with all of his might, but they still trembled.

"I just can't."

His heart worked the inside of his ribcage like a heavyweight fighter hitting a heavy bag. His fingers tingled and he struggled to draw breath.

"This is ridiculous," he said, and he punched the floor. "Five minutes to dress myself and twenty spent trying to convince myself I should walk outside that door."

He shook the sting from his hand and looked at the door. It was thick and heavy.

"Why am I like this?"

He stood, walked to his nightstand and gathered a pen and paper.

"I tried," he said, and he began to write. He offered Anna an apology and a reason why he couldn't go outside. Doing that reminded him of the day the police came to his home and kicked his door down. He hated that memory. The message he'd written didn't do anything to save the lives of the police officers and the many doctors that followed.

Alister folded the note and slipped it underneath the door. He moved to the bed and sat.

Moments later, two light knocks at the door drew Alister's attention, and Anna stepped inside the room. She wore a smile wide enough to show her teeth.

"You smile to cover your disappointment," Alister said, and he looked at the floor.

"Disappointment?" Anna positioned herself next to Alister. "I'm happy you've made it this far. This day has been filled with great progress, and you should be proud and encouraged by it."

Alister returned a saddened smile of his own. "I can't help but feel I let us both down." He turned his gaze to the covered window. "The darkness I've been placed in reminds me of days I would much rather forget."

"That wasn't my intention."

"It's OK," he said. "Maybe it'll encourage me to get out of here."

"I know you'll go when you're ready."

Alister laughed. "The thought of my leaving this room absolutely petrifies me—so much so that I feel physically ill." Alister searched the archives of his mind. "And I can't remember the last time I felt ill."

"Like a cold or flu?"

"Yeah, any of that. It's like I've always been immune, like the curse keeps me healthy. It sounds silly, I know."

Anna fixed a look of confusion on Alister. He watched her turn the chair so that it faced his bed, and she sat. She placed her briefcase on her lap, opened it and shuffled through papers.

"Take a look at these," she said.

Anna handed Alister a few pages.

"What are they?"

Alister looked the pages over.

"They're your medical records," she said. "Do you remember being treated for any of these conditions?"

"No."

Anna sifted through more paperwork and handed Alister another page.

"Do you recognize that?"

"No." It was a photocopy of a handwritten letter.

"That is your handwriting, is it not?"

"Yes, it is."

Anna paused.

"A self-diagnosis of a fever. Swollen glands and, as you state, difficulty breathing."

"I don't remember writing that."

"You requested penicillin as a method of treatment."

"I didn't write that."

"I need you to take a moment to think it through."

"I don't need a moment." He dropped the papers on the bed. "I haven't had so much as a cold since I was a teenager."

Anna returned the pages to her briefcase.

"You wrote those notes to the hospital doctor," Anna said. "You submitted one only three weeks before I arrived and were given the proper medications to treat your illness. I verified this information with the hospital physician and was even allowed to review your file."

"They're fake."

Anna looked at Alister with doubt. "In your own handwriting?"

"I don't know." He scratched his head. "Maybe I was drugged."

"That sounds like a lot of work—and for what?"

"I don't know." His eyes scanned the room in search of an answer. "To confuse me."

"Just so they could show it to me so I could show it to you? So I could convince you the curse wasn't real?"

"I don't know." He sighed, looked away and fingered his beard. "All I know is I didn't write those notes."

Anna searched her briefcase.

"I'm going to leave these with you." She tossed Alister a bottle.

"What are they?"

"For your nerves."

Alister opened the bottle and inspected the contents.

"I want you to take two of them before breakfast."

Alister nodded.

"Discontinue using any meds they've prescribed for you here."

Alister capped the bottle and looked to Anna in question.

"I don't trust them, either," she said. "Something funny is going on here, and I haven't figured out what it is yet."

CHAPTER 21

A TRIP OUTSIDE

Alister sighed and rubbed his eyes. The call of sleep buzzed inside his head, but his mind worked overtime with question and wonder, keeping him anxious and awake. He ran taut fingers through his hair. Anna had said she didn't trust anyone at the hospital, and he couldn't escape the question of why. She had given him new pills to take, and it was done in secrecy.

"What for?"

Alister scratched his head and sat up. "As my doctor, doesn't she have every right to do that?"

He got out of bed and grabbed the bottle of pills. He placed it on the tabletop with the label faced out.

"Prozac."

He grunted and continued to inspect the bottle in search of something that might reveal any trickery. He popped the top, dealt himself two pills and lined them on the tabletop like soldiers that stood at attention. Like a strict drill sergeant, he inspected them. He didn't expect to find skull and crossbones embossed on them, but if he did, he would know they were poisonous and his trust in Anna had been misplaced.

"Nothing," he said. "But I still think it is better for me to trust my own mind rather than one that is drugged and vulnerable to manipulation."

He placed the pills inside the bottle and tossed them on his bed. Although he was consumed with fear and unable to make it outside yesterday, he expected very different results in the morning.

"I can do this."

A sudden surge of confidence filled Alister with energy and made him smile.

"I need to do this."

"If you have any doubts—"

"No. I've had an entire night to work out any doubts."

Anna smiled. "Good."

"Did you make sure nobody else was going to be outside?"

"Yes, as I said yesterday, where we are going, there won't be anyone."

"OK," Alister said. He stood, grabbed his windbreaker and drew a deep breath. He exhaled hard to blow away any doubt that remained. "OK, let's go."

Anna moved to the door. "I'm confident this will bring you closer to an understanding of what I believe plagues you."

"I won't lie," Alister said with a smile. "I'm nervous, but something inside is telling me that the decision I've made to go outside is a must and that something good is about to happen."

"I know that to be true." She pulled the door open and held it. "Move at a pace you're comfortable with. We're in no hurry."

A small lit area of the hallway came into Alister's view, and he swallowed hard.

"I can do this."

He slung his windbreaker on and took a step toward the door. His legs felt as heavy as cement stanchions and his heart went off to the races.

"I'm proud of you, Alister."

Anna's encouragement was background noise to him. He held onto the doorjamb tight and stepped into the hallway. It was bright—much brighter than the darkness of his room—and it hurt his eyes. It was long, too—seeming to go on forever. Sweat ran down his back, and a tremble ran through his entire body. Rows of closed doors spaced every twelve to fifteen feet went on as far as he could see. His last memory of the hallway was a distant blur.

Anna stood far enough away from Alister to allow him freedom to explore.

"There are that many people who are like me?" His firm grip remained on the doorjamb.

"Like you in a sense, but different in many ways." Anna started to walk away.

Alister's hold broke away from the doorjamb with a thump and he took several quick steps toward Anna. He stopped and glanced over his shoulder toward his room. The air left his lungs, and his legs warbled. He bent over and grabbed his knees.

"Hold on," he said, barely audible.

He was about ten feet away from his room, but it could have been a mile. The hallway seemed to stretch and narrow and pull him farther and farther away from his room.

"Are you OK?" Anna said, already by his side.

Alister knelt and felt the sweat that oozed from his pores coat his skin. "I'm fine," he said. Her question chased away the tremble in his body, and he was reminded of the time he tried to be brave and see his grandmother.

"If at anytime you don't feel like you can proceed, you let me know."

"No." He wouldn't allow his emotions to get the better of him. He stood. "I can do this."

Alister moved on in silence at a slow pace, and Anna didn't seem to mind. He took in the details of his surroundings. Bright fluorescent lights reflected off the polished floor. Upholstered loveseats custom fit in alcoves and hand painted pictures of breathtaking landscapes helped create an atmosphere that made one think they were somewhere else other than a mental institution.

"Have you spoken to any of the other patients besides me?" The echo of his voice carried much farther than it had in his room, and what he heard sounded like someone else speaking.

"No," Anna said. "I haven't."

"I think I heard regret in your reply."

"And I can't deny the accuracy of your observation." Her tone was soft. "Of course, I wish I could help them all."

"So why me?" Alister stopped walking and his sneaker screeched. "I mean out of all these people, why did I get you?"

Anna shrugged. "I don't know. Maybe someone was looking out for you, and it was just your time."

"Yeah, maybe it was."

Alister wore a smile as he walked with Anna through the long hallway. Captivated by the details of the paintings, he allowed himself to drift in thought and imagine that he was standing on the bridge he saw and looking down into the clear water.

He continued on, looking into the small windows on the doors. None of them were covered like his had been. People were huddled in the corners of their rooms. Some of them screamed at things unseen and others were oblivious to the eyes that watched them. They were trapped inside the confines of their own minds, keeping company with madness.

Alister scratched an itch on his arm that traveled to his scalp and attempted to hide in the tangle of hair on top of his head.

Anna paused in front of a door that had an illuminated exit sign above it. Beyond the glass sidelights, a walkway arranged with red pavers surrounded by colorful flowers and small bushes with bright green leaves could be seen. A few life-sized statues guarded the way, and in the center of a roundabout was a tall fountain releasing a cascade of water that glistened in the sunlight.

"Are you doing OK?"

Alister's gaze remained transfixed. The bright greens, yellows and reds were vivid and unfamiliar.

"I..." His jaw quivered. "The brown...." He licked his lips. "The reach of death hasn't come this far. I don't remember things being this beautiful."

Anna exited the building and held the door for Alister.

A strong breeze that carried a chill and the smell of flowers gave Alister goose bumps and filled his senses. The sky was clear and the air was crisp. He stepped outside, drew a deep breath and held it. He felt as though he had inhaled new life, and he didn't want to let it go. He had breathed stale indoor air for over twenty years, and the first breath he had taken of the outdoors was like rich chocolate on his taste buds. Alister closed his eyes and relaxed his shoulders and mind.

"Heaven."

Anna took Alister by the hand. Her touch was gentle on the lumpy flesh of his palms. "Come," she said. "I have a special place for us to sit. It's a place even more beautiful than this."

"Your hands are cold," Alister said. The chill ran deep enough to penetrate the thick layer of scar tissue on his hands. "And it is chilly out, so here. Take my jacket."

"That's very kind of you, Alister, but I'm fine."

Anna wore a skirt and a light blouse.

"I insist." He started to remove his jacket.

"I'm fine, thank you."

Birds chirped, and Alister tried to find them among the tall, healthy trees. When he spotted one, he stopped walking and stared at it.

"What's wrong?" Anna said.

The bird ran back and forth on the branch, bobbed its head, jumped from its perch and flew away. Alister watched it until it disappeared into the distance.

"Nothing," he said. "Nothing at all."

Anna led Alister past the roundabout and down a path that gave way to a lush garden. Marble benches were positioned in the corners and a thick outlying forest bordered the garden.

Anna sat on one of the benches, and Alister explored the area with his eyes. He remained close to Anna's side like a child afraid to stray too far from his mother's protective reach.

"It is nice here," Alister said.

"Yes, it is."

"I don't know." He turned toward the roundabout. "I feel like I should go back inside before the death that follows me starts to destroy it."

Anna pointed at a row of low windows. "Do you see those windows?"

Alister looked. "Yes."

"The second window to the end is your room. I had them remove the boards when we left."

Alister pointed toward the window. "There?" He looked to Anna and then over his shoulder and down the path they had emerged from. "No." He scratched his head and looked back to the window. "I live on the other side."

"I think you should go to the window and have a look inside. If you see for yourself, then you'll understand that I'm not trying to trick you."

Alister was hesitant, but he went. He grabbed hold of the cold steel bars and peered inside the room. It was all as he had kept it. He looked back to the lush garden.

"This isn't how I've seen things for the past twenty years."

"I know how hard this must be for you, Alister, but this is what you've been looking at," Anna said.

Alister was fascinated by the way the flowers were tilted toward the sun. And one yellow flower located in the center of the garden drew his attention and held it.

"Why don't we sit down and talk about what you're feeling?"

Alister flinched. He didn't notice Anna's approach.

"What I'm feeling?" He shook his head in an attempt to chase away the cloud of confusion that whirled inside his mind. "Before you had my windows covered, everything outside my room was dead. The only thing alive was that flower." He looked to the spot where he had seen it. "But it wasn't here, it was from a dream."

Anna encouraged Alister along with a gentle tug on his sleeve. "Come on."

"But it was just a dream," Alister said.

They moved to the bench and sat.

"That flower I saw—it was big and yellow and stretched toward the sun."

"I had your windows covered because I believed your mind was showing you things that weren't really there."

Alister leaned forward and rested his elbows on his knees. "So there it is—validation that I'm as crazy as everyone else in Sunnyside."

"The first time you were telling me about the decay of the garden, I was standing behind you and looking out with you. I was seeing the beauty that is in front of you right now."

"No, the things outside my window were dead."

"There weren't any dead plants or trees. There were beautiful greens, yellows and reds. Exactly what you see here."

"No, there weren't."

"I knew the importance of creating separation between you and the things you were identifying with the curse."

"I'm telling you that there was death as far as my eyes could see."

"I believed if I reintroduced you to the garden without you realizing it was the same thing you'd been looking at, then your mind wouldn't create the same depressing imagery."

Alister broke his stare from the garden, and looked to Anna. "Am I crazy?"

"You've lived through heavy trauma. That disturbance has forced your mind to create a reality within itself to try and shield you."

"What trauma, doctor?"

"One step at a time, Alister."

She took Alister's hand. "To answer your question, no, I don't think you're crazy, because if you were, you wouldn't have comprehended the things I've just told you."

Alister wiped his eyes. "I'm so confused."

Anna stood and placed a hand on his shoulder.

"How am I supposed to know the difference between what is real and what isn't?" Alister asked.

"Time," Anna said, and she hugged him.

"The things you say happened are things I can't remember happening."

"The only thing you need to remember right now is that I will be around as long as it takes."

"The dream seemed so real. That lone flower bursting with life, living in the middle of all the decay outside my window."

Alister pointed to the flower.

"It was that one. Moments after I spotted the flower, you brought my uncle into the room. The only problem with that is that he's been dead for years."

"Do you want to know what I think?"

Alister looked at Anna with eyes that begged for an answer.

"I think that dream you had was trying to tell you something. I believe your life was a representation of that flower, and if it can endure and survive in such an unwelcoming environment, well then, so can you."

Alister smiled but deeply doubted it.

"The bad thoughts you have are the product of your own creation," Anna said. "Yes, you are sick, but not incurable."

Alister whimpered, got down on his knees and hugged Anna by her waist. She was thin and seemed delicate, but he knew she was filled with the strength and the know-how of ten people.

"Please, don't ever leave me," he said, and he squeezed her tight.

"It'll be OK," Anna said. "Let's go inside. There is something else I need to show you."

"Alister?"

"Yes?"

He was in his room, and there were two people that looked back at him with hopeful eyes. One of the people was Anna, but he didn't recognize the other person. "Who is he?" Alister asked.

"You can hear me?" the strange man asked.

Somehow Alister knew that voice and instantly found comfort in it.

"Of course I can hear you."

A boy that was barely a man stood with Anna, and his eyes were wet and red.

"Do you think he knows who I am?" the man asked. His voice trembled.

"Yes, I believe he does," Anna said.

"Thank you," the man said, and he cried hard.

"Please," Alister said. "Don't you ever cry for me again." The sadness in the man's eyes broke his heart. He reached out and stroked the man's cheek. "I'm not sure what I've done to you, but I'm certain it was bad. I'm sorry for the pain I've caused you and hope you know I wouldn't have done those things if I were in control."

Alister didn't know why he said those things, but it needed to be said.

"I know," the man said, and he wiped his tears.

Alister reached out and pulled him close. He tapped his temple. "I'm well aware that things inside here haven't been right for a long time. I've tried to fight it, but it lives in here." Alister pouted. "I also know that I'm better off here."

"Alister?"

Alister looked at Anna.

"Who are you talking to?"

Alister's hands held onto something that wasn't there. The man that stood within his grasp a moment before was no longer present. He lowered his hands and moved to the window. "I'm not sure."

"Are you OK?" Anna asked.

"I'm fine."

Anna reached out to touch him. "Alister?"

"I'm fine. I mean it," he said as he shied away.

Alister snuck a glance over his shoulder and saw Anna searching through her briefcase.

"It just seemed like your mind was somewhere else for a minute."

Crazy bastard.

"No, I've been here the entire time."

"As long as you're OK," Anna said, and she removed papers from her briefcase. She tapped them on the tabletop to neaten the stack.

Crazy bastard.

"What?" Alister said.

I said you are crazy.

"I am," Alister said to both his inner voice and to Anna.

"OK," Anna said.

"I just have a million uncertainties hanging over me like a black cloud."

"Do you hate clichés?"

"I do."

"Then I don't need to tell you about Rome and a day?"

"No." Alister smiled. He moved to the unmade bed and sat.

"Your Grandmother Dotsy," Anna said. She walked around the bed and stood in front of Alister. "She died three years before you were born."

Alister stared at Anna. "What did you say?" He interlaced his fingers and placed his hands in his lap. "That's ridiculous. It's true."

"No," Alister said. "It's not." He fixed his eyes on Anna in a defiant stare. "I won't let you do this."

"Everything I'm telling you is in truth."

Alister stood and clenched his fists. He wanted to scream, hit something and cause someone pain just so they would know how he felt.

"I won't do it. I won't let these stories confuse me. I know what is real." He flexed his hands and drew a deep breath. He sat. "I know what is real," Alister said, and his voice trailed off.

"I want you to look at this," Anna said. She handed Alister a document that was old and carried a musty smell.

Alister took the paper but held it away. The memories of his grandmother were fresh and real, and for the doctor to tell him it was something he had imagined not only insulted him but also provoked his temper.

"Please, read it."

The parchment was yellowed and brittle. The ink was faded but legible. It was a death certificate.

"No," Alister said. "I clearly remember going to her house after school. She used to help me with my homework and feed me dinner."

"No, she didn't. It is as the paper states. She died before you were born."

CHAPTER 22

HURT HANDS

The past.

A flash of pain that surrounded Alister's elbow woke him from a deep sleep. He groaned and rubbed at the throbbing, trying to remember what had made him thrash.

"Death," he said, his resonating voice a dull echo. He licked his dry cracked lips with a tongue coated with saliva so thick that it was like paste. "You've taken them all from me. Do you need to cause me pain as a reminder that you're still around me?"

Death had come for every one of his family members, and he could do nothing but watch their struggle. They tried to run from the shadowy faceless figure in a ragged cloak. It had eyes that glowed red and a deep, taunting laugh. Sometimes its approach was fast, but most of the time it would take its time and make people suffer. And in the end, death always got its fill.

Shadowy tendrils that reached down from the ceiling commanded Alister's attention. The way they swayed were like fingers of a skeletal hand reaching out, and that made him forget the pain in his elbow and the contents of his dream.

"What is that?"

Alister rubbed his eyes. Cobwebs that weighed down by dust and debris waved in the draft.

"Strange. My eyes must be adjusting to the darkness."

He had lost count of how many days he had been locked inside the small room. His internal clock told him it had been over ninety-six hours.

"Four days."

He yawned, stretched and sat up. He looked behind himself, and the door to the room was ajar. A small wedge of light was beaming through.

He rushed to his feet and grunted at the stiffness that had settled in his joints.

"Four days of living in my own filth—"

He moved to the door, and though tempted to close it and remain within the safety of the room, he knew he couldn't. The security of the room had been compromised.

"—for nothing."

He shifted on his feet and spied what was beyond the room.

Dozens of chairs were stacked, one on top of the other. Odd items were strewn about, and filing cabinets and office desks were piled without care.

Alister moved forward and was stopped by something that snagged his shirt. The steel on the door had been peeled inward and sharp shards stuck out in all directions.

"So now what am I supposed to do?" someone said in the room beyond his.

Alister moved away. His blood warmed and indecision raced through his mind.

"I've arranged everything as you instructed."

Alister tried to push the door closed, but it wouldn't budge.

"I'm ready to go whenever you are."

Alister looked at the man with bulging muscles. His eyes were so red they appeared to glow. Just like death's did.

"How much longer do you need?" Milos asked.

"Where are we going?"

"Don't you remember?"

As big as that man was, he looked pathetic and weak.

"Remember what?"

"Coming to me last night?"

Alister shook his head. "No."

"Are you telling me you can't feel that?"

Alister exited the room and stood next to a stack of desks. The floor was dirt, and each step stirred dust.

"What are you talking about?"

"Look at your hands."

Deep lacerations covered both hands. The wounds were jagged and filled with dried blood and grime.

"My God," Alister said, and he looked at the door.

"That door was intact when we put you inside that room."

Alister opened and closed his hands. They felt stiff but there was no pain. "I don't understand."

"When you came to me last night, I was sleeping by that desk." He pointed at two desks that had been placed upright and butted together. "You tapped me on my shoulder, and I thought I was dreaming. That's when you grabbed me, shook me, and got real close to me and said, 'Boo.'"

"You didn't hear me trying to get out?" Alister ran his fingertips over the serrated metal.

The muscleman shook his head. "I've been keeping watch over you for days making sure you couldn't get out of that room. But when you got out, I tried to get away from you. But you grabbed my arm and held me still without a problem." He moved close to Alister and lifted his sleeve. In a clear purple bruise he could see a handprint. "I couldn't believe how strong you were, and no matter how hard I tried pulling away, I couldn't loosen your hold."

Alister felt small next to Milos.

"You told me you were hungry and thirsty and that you would be waiting for your meal in the room and that I shouldn't keep you waiting."

Alister looked away. "I don't remember any of this."

"When I brought you your meal, you were sitting in the center of the room. Your hands were dripping with blood and that is when I noticed how you had gotten out of the room. I offered you assistance with your wounds, but you denied me, taking only the food and water."

"How long ago?"

"Several hours."

"I don't think you have much time."

"Yes, I realize that. You instructed me to arrange a place where you would be away from human contact, but also a place where necessities would be provided for you every day. I've made such arrangements. We should go now."

CHAPTER 23

A NEW MAN

Present day.

Alister pinched a clump of chin hair between his pointer finger and thumb and pulled it tight. He held scissors as close to the skin as possible and cut the hair from his beard, dropping the clippings into the sink. When he cut away all the length, he wet his face and lathered it with soap, using extra care to shave away the remaining stubble.

The coolness of the air that touched his newly exposed skin tingled. He used his fingertips to trace his soft jawline, which was sensitive to the touch. And when he gazed into the mirror, an unfamiliar stranger looked back at him.

I haven't seen you in a long time. Welcome back.

Alister moved to the shower stall and turned on the water. The showerhead belched, gurgled and spat a weak stream of rusted water. Once the water cleared, he adjusted the temperature to his liking and disrobed. He grabbed the bar of soap off of the sink and stepped into the shower. He settled beneath the warm jet of water that soaked his body. The thought that layers of grime were being peeled away and a new person was emerging made him eager to clean himself. He was gentle with the soap at first, but his need to escape what he had been for so long brought about an intensity that encouraged him to move faster, scrub harder.

When he stepped out of the shower, Alister whistled as he moved about, grabbing a plush towel and drying his body off. The door to his room swung open and Michael hobbled in.

"Good morning," Alister said.

Michael made no attempt to make eye contact with Alister and muttered his response. "Good morning."

Alister wrapped his body with the towel and stepped out of the bathroom. He had hoped to share his new look and relish in a moment of surprise and compliments.

"Are you OK?" Alister said.

"Just tired." Michael looked at Alister and forced a smile. "You showered and shaved; you look like you're ready to take on the world."

"Thank you."

The deep purple rings surrounding Michael's eyes didn't escape Alister's notice.

"Are you sure you're OK?"

"I'm fine."

"You don't seem to be fine."

"Listen, I would love to stay and chat, but I have a million things to do."

Alister nodded his understanding. "Yeah, OK." He looked at his chair and the wear in the fabric was a good comparison to how Michael looked. His shoulders were slumped and his eyes watched his feet. His face grimaced with each step he took, and when he grabbed the door handle, he rested his head against the wall.

"You should know that you look good, Alister. You really do. And I'm glad that you are feeling better. I see a big improvement within you. I really do."

Michael sighed and exited the room.

CHAPTER 24

PRESENTING: THE TRUTH

Anna reached out and touched Alister's shaven face.

"I think it has taken away at least ten years." She raised her brows and a smile overtook her face. "You clean up well."

Alister's smile matched Anna's. "Thank you."

"You're welcome."

"I'm sure anything I did would be an improvement from how I looked before."

"Give yourself a little more credit than that."

Alister looked at the vibrant plant life beyond his window. Everything looked so peaceful and inviting. "I enjoyed yesterday."

"I did too, and I'm proud of you."

He patted his chest. "I don't know what it did to me, but something inside has changed."

Anna moved beside him and pointed to the variety of color in the garden. "So you can still see the beauty?"

He moved his face close to the window, and when he spoke, the glass fogged from the heat of his breath. "I want to go back outside."

"Then grab your jacket."

After Alister put on a second layer of clothes, they exited his room and walked down the hallway. Alister took his time and inspected everything he had seen the day before. With curious eyes, he looked through the small windows of each door, and the people he saw inside their rooms sat motionless in front of their windows overlooking the garden.

"Just like me."

He believed that the constant longing that filled their hearts eventually flattened their hope. He knew that because he had done that every day for as long as he could remember. But he would no longer wait for that void to be filled by something that would never come. He snickered at the thought.

"Maybe I have made progress."

There was a world outside his small room, and it waited to share its beauty and reveal something special to him.

"I won't do it—not anymore," he said, and he turned away from the rooms. He followed Anna outside the hospital in silent contemplation as they made their way to the bench that overlooked the garden.

The splendor of the day was spectacular. Each breath Alister drew was deep and carried the scent of fresh cut grass and flowers that had flourished in the bright day's sun.

"Beautiful."

The air was crisp and refreshing.

Anna watched Alister and smiled at his joy.

"You have given me hope for the future I never thought possible," Alister said. He sat on the bench next to Anna. He leaned back and gave pause to soak in the beauty that surrounded him. Tall trees, green grass, blooming flowers and puffy white clouds against a powder blue backdrop made him feel alive. "I quit on you yesterday, and I'm sorry for it."

"Your successes, no matter how big or small, never require an apology."

Alister studied Anna. Her inner and outer beauty complimented the moment perfectly.

"You told me you had had enough, and that is what you're supposed to do," she said.

"I think I'm ready for whatever else you have to tell me."

It was Anna's turn to study Alister's face. "You're certain of this?" Her eyes searched his for any sign of doubt.

Alister smiled. "You're doing it again, doctor, but not as badly as you did when we first met."

Anna cracked a smile, nodded her understanding and leaned back. A cool breeze lifted her hair gently and her nose was reddened at the tip.

Alister could smell the scent of her shampoo, and he was reminded of Sharon. He inhaled, held his breath and closed his eyes.

"Tell me what you remember about your father."

Alister opened one eye and trained it on Anna. "He was a kind man that worked very hard to support us. And I remember whenever he came home from work he would be whistling or singing. Dad was good to Mom, and they were always a lot of fun together."

Anna nodded as Alister spoke, and it seemed odd that she wasn't gripping a pen and taking notes.

"And tell me some things about your mother," she said.

"She was a perfect woman," Alister said. "I've compared every woman that I've ever met to her, and none have come close—not even my wife. You know, you remind me of my mother in a lot of ways."

"How so?" Anna said. Her eyes were wide with curiosity.

"Well, for starters, she was the most beautiful woman in the world. And like you, she had a genuine care for the people she came in contact with."

Anna bobbed her head at the compliment and fought away the smile that had parted her lips. "Can you tell me anything negative you might remember about them?"

Alister sighed and struggled as he searched for something to say. "Well, my mother was weakened a lot by her dependency on religion. I also didn't get to see them as much as I would have liked. Several hours after I got home from school, they would pick me up from my grand—"

Alister licked his lips and fell silent. His rosy cheeks hid the rush of embarrassment he felt burn his face.

"What is it?"

"If everything I knew about my grandmother was a lie, then what about my parents? That's what this is about, isn't it?"

Anna nodded with a solemn expression on her face.

"What is the truth about them then?"

She paused before she turned askew, her full attention on Alister. A gentle concern filled her eyes and her hand moved to his knees. "When you were seven years old, you witnessed your mother drowning your younger brother in the bathtub after she had killed your father."

Alister watched the bright day turn black before his very eyes. He searched Anna's eyes for the lie she had just told him. But nothing but compassion could be seen. "I don't have a brother."

"You were at a friend's house for dinner that day. When you came home and no one answered your calls, you heard noise coming from the upstairs bathroom. When you went up there, you found your father facedown in a pool of blood."

"Becca."

"You saw your mother kneeling over the bathtub, holding something that was struggling against her grasp underneath the water, splashing violently."

"My wife." He shook his head and searched for the memory. Death and the curse were all he could find. "I don't have a brother."

"What you were reported saying to an investigating officer was that your mother looked at you as if she were serving dinner, holding casual conversation and asking you to come to her. You were smart enough to sense the danger you were in and ran to a neighbor's house."

"I don't have a brother."

"When the authorities got to your house, they found your mother had committed suicide."

"I don't have a brother."

Anna lifted Alister's chin with a gentle hand and forced his eyes to meet hers. "You did."

"I didn't."

Anna didn't respond.

"I left him to die?"

Anna pulled him close and held him strong. "You were just a kid, Alister. You can't blame yourself for your mother's behavior. She was a sick woman that abused you and your brother. Your father tried to keep you from her rage, but he couldn't be there all the time. And those days, it was taboo for outsiders to interfere in anyone's family affairs."

"What was my brother's name?"

"Brett."

"Brett," Alister said. The hum of an electric motor approaching halted his thought. He watched Michael drive by in a golf cart. He was towing a small cart that was covered by a tarp.

CHAPTER 25

THE LAST LAUGH

The past.

"I forget your name," Alister said, and he winced. He watched the muscleman clean the deep cuts on his palms.

"Milos," he said. "Am I hurting you?"

"No," Alister said, and he tried to place Milos' accent. "What happened to your friends is what hurts."

Milos paused then got back to cleaning the cuts.

"You don't have to say anything," Alister said. "I know what you're feeling because I've had to live it every day."

Milos continued to work without pause.

"And the hurt I feel will never go away. After you die, there will be another."

Milos placed white medical tape over the gauze. "I'd prefer we didn't talk about it."

"There is always another."

Milos slapped Alister's knee. "There, that should do it."

"You're Hispanic."

"What?"

"I'm trying to place your accent."

"I'm Portuguese."

"I never would have gotten that."

Alister squeezed and opened his hand. The pain was intense.

"We should get going," Milos said. "There are a lot of people I had to put in place to make this work. They're all awaiting your arrival."

"And they all know what they need to know about me?"

"Yes. Follow me."

Milos led Alister through hallways lined with pipes and lit with dim pigtail lights that blinked. They walked up two flights of steps and out a steel door that squealed when it opened. Alister took two steps outside and climbed into the back of a parked van.

"Where am I being taken?"

Milos sat in the driver's seat and turned to face Alister. He faced forward and started the van.

"You are being taken to a facility called Sunnyside Capable Care Mental Institution. It's a hospital, and you'll be given a private room similar to solitary confinement in prison. You'll be given three squares a day, and all necessities will be provided."

Inside the van, the back and side windows were covered with cardboard and duct tape. Alister subconsciously fought the sway of the vehicle while his mind was immersed in a distant possibility. "Maybe I have a chance of beating this thing."

Milos nodded. "I hope so." Blood trickled from his nose. He wiped the blood away and pressed the gas pedal. The engine revved, and the vehicle lurched forward. "It seems this is the beginning of the end for me."

Alister could see his worry. "I'm sorry."

"Don't be."

Milos jerked the van to a sudden halt, turned around in his seat and looked at Alister. "I hope to be back in a minute so I can finish this." He got out of the van. "Wait here." He slammed the door shut and ran away.

Out of the front window of the van, Alister watched a man dressed in all white run toward him. He was pushing a wheelchair.

"No," Alister said. Sorrow settled in his chest and wrapped his heart. "Why are you doing this to me?" he asked the curse.

The side door of the van slid open, and the man waited for Alister without word or eye contact.

Alister exited the van and sat in the wheelchair. He was pushed across the parking lot and into the side entrance of a building he had no doubt was the hospital Milos had mentioned.

An entourage of people waited and whispered until Alister neared. As if each move were rehearsed, he was moved through long, bright hallways. The floors were polished to a high gloss, the ceilings and walls were a sterile white and doors with small windows were lined one after the other. Distant, muffled shouts of torment gave the hospital an ominous feel.

They rounded a corner, and there was a woman in a wheelchair speaking to someone that couldn't be seen by others. She was being pushed down the hallway toward Alister as her babble grew louder. A wild, distant stare accompanied her rant, and her focus became fixated on Alister.

"You," the insane woman said. Her eyes filled with rage, and she pointed a bent finger at him. "You reap what you sow!"

She jumped out of her chair, and before anyone could react, she was on top of Alister. She raked her fingernails across his face and slapped him.

"You wonder why you're being pursued by that invisible demon when you're the one who invited it in?"

Alister tried to protect himself, but the blows kept coming.

"Get her off of me!"

But they had already gotten her back in her wheelchair. Everyone had stopped and looked at him.

"What have you done?" a man with a crooked nose asked Alister. He was dressed in a suit and tie rather than a white doctor's uniform like everyone else.

"I..."

"Why would you?" the man asked. If Alister had gotten to know him, he would have known him as Director Lofton.

"I'm sorry," Alister said.

"Get him into his room now before he infects someone else."

"My God," Alister said, and he looked at all the people that were there. "What have I done?"

"Murderer," the insane woman said. Her accusation was loud, clear and true.

Alister stood up from the wheelchair and walked to his room. "I'm sorry," he said as he closed the door. He rested his forehead against the door. "For whatever it's worth, I'm sorry."

CHAPTER 26

DEATH PERCEPTION

Present day.

"I don't understand," Anna said. Her arms were held wide in question, and her eyes were bright with wonder. "Why in the world would you purposely invite a curse into your life?"

"You're trying to simplify something that is complicated. My having to deal with the death of pets as a child and kneel beside friends and family as they lay in caskets as I got older brought about a search for the meaning of life."

"Questions like why we are here?"

"Yes. And my mother's obsession with religion and the nonresponses she would get after years of devout prayer encouraged a change in me that had me searching everywhere but heavenward."

"So you're angry at God?"

"With each death I had to mourn, my focus became fixated on the idea that something other than God had control over our destinies."

Alister snickered, shook his head and looked away.

"I'm sure this all sounds so very dramatic to a mental health doctor," Alister said. "But as hard as my mother would pray, she never got one single request answered, and yet day after day she would get on her knees and thank God for anything and everything that happened in her life."

"And this angered you. Why?"

"Good or bad, it didn't matter," Alister said. "She was thankful and submissive, and I could never

156

understand why. I surmised that having to suffer one way or another was what we were designed to endure. Whether from self-persecution or the mean nature of others, it didn't matter. So why in the world should God be given thanks for that?"

"What I don't understand," Anna said, "is why, when things get tough for someone, do they immediately blame God? I mean do people really think they are so important that they feel God owes them something?"

"If God is all-knowing and all-powerful, then He has the ability to change things and make them right, but He doesn't."

"Then what about free will?"

"Let's not forget about all the disease that can riddle our bodies, tragic accidents that plague our days and random acts of violence we commit against each other because we are made in His likeness."

Alister stood and started to walk the path toward the roundabout, and Anna followed.

"And one night while I mourned the loss of my grandmother, the idea that death was not just an event that was going to happen but, that it must have been controlled by someone consumed me, and I was compelled to communicate with it. I believed if I could gain its mercy and trust, I could escape its wrath and wouldn't have to suffer the same fate as everyone else I knew. So I prayed to death every night for mercy to spare me from the suffering I had had to witness."

"Is that what this is about?" Anna's tone was gentle. "Are you afraid to die, Alister?"

Alister rubbed his chin and could feel stubble that had grown back. "I used to be when I was much younger, but not anymore. I would welcome it if there were a way." Alister stopped at the roundabout and looked down the path that would bring him back to his room. He turned away from that route. "Let us not go back to my room just yet."

Anna stopped by Alister's side and refrained from making any comment or suggestion.

"I believe it was after the very first time I prayed I had gotten a response. I felt a void fill that had been empty for a long time. And right then I knew I was onto something. I had already gotten a greater response than my mother had, and that proved my prayers were being heard."

"And you prayed to death?"

"Yes, to the entity that was responsible for it."

Alister looked down the path that bent alongside the entire length of the hospital. On one side, the enormous building stretched toward the sky, and on the other side, the thick forest blocked out most of the sunlight.

Alister pointed into the distance toward the front of the hospital. "I haven't been down that way. Do you mind taking a walk?"

Anna hesitated. "Let's not roam too far. I've only secured this area of the building."

"I don't mind." Alister started on the path and examined his surroundings as he moved onward. "But this is interesting." He eyed the trees and rubbed his chin.

"What?"

Alister held up a finger and prompted Anna's silence. "You know, the idea that I'd discovered death was an actual living, thinking being filled me with a range of emotions that went from absolute fear to adoration and even to curiosity. To imagine such a being to be real was incomprehensible, and I wondered if it could be labeled as good or evil—good because it ended people's suffering and evil because it was designed to end someone's life."

"You sound sympathetic to it."

"Did it perform its task with malice, or did it find remorse within the parameters of its lonely existence?"

Anna clasped her hands behind her back. "This is interesting, but it is nothing more than forged memories to protect you."

Alister kept his focus on the tree line. "What I really wanted to know was how it would respond to love—even admiration—from someone that was supposed to fear it."

"Alister?"

"But could you imagine?" Alister asked, his face bright with excitement. "Imagine how I felt when death began to show me favor. I felt as though I'd discovered eternal life—the key to living forever. I celebrated the idea that I was immune to illness, injury and, ultimately, death."

"Alister."

"But everything has a price," Alister said. "Death was jealous and filled with such rage that it wouldn't allow anyone near me. It was as though I had become its possession and no one was permitted around me."

"Why are you telling me this again?"

"And it wouldn't allow me happiness."

"I thought we moved past this."

"And no matter what elaborate plan I tried to create to escape it, it would punish me by lashing out against those around me."

Alister stopped walking and placed his hands on his hips. "As time went on, my misery only deepened, and the deaths started becoming more frequent and increasingly violent. With all of my family gone, I knew I had to get away to preserve as much life as possible. And that, doctor, is how I ended up here in Sunnyside."

Alister looked at Anna and searched for the truth. "And suddenly I think I get it."

"Get what?"

"That you are death."

Anna stiffened. "You've got to be kidding me."

"Just take a moment and tell me what you hear."

Alister fell silent and rocked on his heels as he waited.

"And what am I supposed to be listening for?"

"Just tell me what you hear."

Anna fell silent. "I don't hear anything."

"Yeah, I noticed the silence when we were sitting on the bench. You underestimated my ability to notice all the birds were gone."

"The direction of this conversation has become absurd," Anna said. "I'm not comfortable with it."

"I suspected that you were death after you returned the second day, but your persistence fooled me."

Anna grabbed Alister's elbow and spun him around. "If I'm death as you claim, how do you explain Michael being alive?"

Alister shrugged. "Last time I saw him, he didn't look well. And that first day we went outside, the birds were chirping and I even saw a bird fly out of a tree. The breeze rustled the leaves and everything felt so alive and clean." Alister looked around. "It was fresh." He started to walk. "But today everything seems so," he said, settling his gaze on Anna, "dead."

Anna crossed her arms. "Look," she said.

"No, you look. I know what you are and what you've done, so why don't you stop playing with me?"

"You seriously can't believe what you're saying."

"Just stop it, OK?" His fists were clenched and his eyes were filled with anger. "Don't treat me like I'm stupid." He turned away to try and hide what stirred within. "I need you to come clean so I can deal with this. That void I spoke to you about, the one that was filled? Well, since your arrival, that feeling has only intensified."

Anna raised a brow. "I would like to respond to you without you telling me I'm lying or having you so insistent that you completely shut down. If you would like, I could just agree with you so you can believe this fantasy is real. If that is what you want, then you can lock yourself away from the rest of the world forever, and I will leave you alone."

Alister pursed his lips and fought against his frustration.

"You need to learn how to listen to me."

Alister crossed his arms and searched for the breeze, but there wasn't one.

"You need to know it's common for a patient to develop feelings for their doctors that care for them. And I will never admit to anything that isn't true."

Alister reached out and brushed his fingers across Anna's cheek. "How come your skin is always ice-cold?"

Anna sighed and resisted a shiver. "Where are the words to answer you?"

"I'm sure you'll find them." He pointed farther down the path that led to the front of the hospital. The air was thick with a haze he hadn't noticed before. "I would like to go that way." And carried a horrible smell. "Maybe I'll be lucky enough to meet some of the people that work here."

Anna hesitated, and Alister saw it. He kept on the path and left her behind.

"Alister!" she said. "You asked that I keep everyone away and now you are in search of someone? They won't be out here per your request."

"You mean to tell me you've shut down the entire operation of a hospital so I can go outside?" Alister said, and he placed his hands over his heart. "I'm really flattered, doctor. Thank you."

Anna closed her eyes and sighed.

"What is it you're so afraid of me finding?" Alister said. "You go to extremes to get me outside to see the beauty that is beyond my room, and now that I want to see things, you resist me. What's around the front of the hospital?"

"Nothing," Anna said. She submitted herself to follow Alister with a sigh. "I'm concerned about your behavior. Have you taken the medicine like I've instructed?"

Alister sniffed the air and looked to Anna in question. "Tell me you smell that."

"Alister? I asked you a question. Have you taken your medication?"

Alister drew in a deep breath and tried to identify the smell that stained the air. "What in the hell is that?"

Anna drew a deep breath. "I don't smell anything."

A distant crackling sound interrupted Alister's investigation and pulled him forward. "This way." He quickened his pace toward the front of the hospital. "That sounds like something is on fire."

He rounded the corner and faced bright orange, blue and yellow flames that raged from an intense bonfire. The flames belched smoke and soot that gushed upward in a toxic puff. The golf cart he had seen Michael drive by in was parked near the blaze. The tarp that covered the cart it was towing was pulled away, and a pile of human and animal carcasses sat in plain sight.

Alister's mouth hung open as he watched Michael carry bodies from the cart and struggle to place them on the fire without burning himself. He looked over his shoulder at Anna and pointed at what he saw. "What is he doing?"

Anna searched the area Alister pointed toward. "What is it, Alister? What do you see?"

An intense anger burning as brightly as the bonfire raged inside Alister. Either Anna was completely blind, or she was playing stupid.

"Don't give me that shit," he said. "What is with that big fucking fire and all the bodies Michael is burning?"

"You need to calm down," Anna said, and she looked to see if she could find what Alister claimed to see. "There is no fire."

Alister could see the blaze reflecting inside Anna's eyes. "What do you mean there is no fire?" He jabbed his finger in the air and stomped his foot with each word. "It is right there in front of you! Are you blind?"

Anna backed away and withdrew a small remote control from her pocket. She pressed a button on the remote. "We need to go back inside so you can calm down."

"I'm not going anywhere with you." He took a step away.

"This was a mistake. I shouldn't have pushed you to do this."

Alister held his hands out toward the fire. "How can you tell me to calm down when I can feel the heat from here?"

"I think it's best if we just get you back to your room now."

Alister looked at Anna with disdain. "What are you trying to do to me? You tell me stories and lie to me—for what?"

Two male orderlies emerged from the hospital and took a hold of Alister by the arms.

"Get your hands off of me!" Alister said, and he struggled to break free from the firm hands that bound him.

"Please get the patient back to his room," Anna said. She visibly trembled and seemed winded. "And please have him restrained to the bed."

"Restrained?" Alister said. "Go ahead—that won't keep me from finding out the truth."

"Relax," one of the orderlies said, and Alister knew it was Michael. Alister no longer struggled against his hold and looked at Michael. "You've got to help me. She's driving me mad."

"Not another word," Michael said. His command was like that of a disappointed parent disciplining their child. "You are doing this to yourself."

He guided Alister down the path and back inside his room.

Alister sat on his bed, the confusion inside his mind as thick as the smoke outside. "Are you going to tell me I didn't see that fire and all those bodies you were burning?"

Michael laid Alister flat on the bed and started to secure restraints to his wrists, waist and ankles. "I believe that you believe that what you say is the truth. But that doesn't always make it so."

"How about you?" Alister said to the other orderly as the straps being tightened around his body pinched his skin and cut off his circulation. "Are you standing by his story?"

"Sir," the orderly said, "you should know we're not qualified to help you with your condition. You need to communicate your concerns to your doctor."

"I see," Alister said. A tear of frustration rolled from the corner of his eye. "But before you go, if you would be so kind to explain why I can smell the smoke on your clothing?"

The past.

Alister stood three feet away from his window and watched a group of hospital patients monitored by three staff members. Although he longed to be out there with them, he knew it was impossible. The curse wouldn't allow it.

The patients worked in the garden, and that was how they were rewarded for their compliance and good behavior. For hours, they would cultivate the land, pull weeds and plant annuals.

It had been nearly two weeks since Alister arrived at Sunnyside Capable Care, and he hadn't spoken to anyone since the crazy woman attacked him. Three meals arrived every day at precise times, and the staff members that entered his room kept quiet, kept their distance and moved with haste.

A large man that wore overalls held Alister's attention. There was no question that he was a patient. He had been on his knees for a long time and took small mounds of dirt out of a hole with a hand shovel. His bright red face dripped with sweat. He suddenly paused in his work. He raised his eyes and looked to Alister.

Alister took two steps back, and his eyes remained on the large man. There was no way he could have seen Alister. The bright day's sun would have made it impossible to see into his dark room.

But the large man stood and waved at Alister, and Alister sat on his bed. There is no way he would offer the curse any opportunity to get anyone ever again.

The large man wiped his brow, tugged on his pant legs and knelt again. He returned his attention to the hole in the ground.

CHAPTER 27

ANSWERED PRAYER

"I believe you can hear me," Alister said into the darkened room. His voice sounded flat, and it faded quickly. "I believed you heard me the first day I prayed to you." He knelt in the center of the room and waited for a response to his declaration.

"That's okay," he said after a brief moment of silence, his voice dropping to a whisper. "I am a patient man and humble enough to know you don't owe me anything in return for what I have to offer you."

A thump in the corner of the room demanded Alister's attention, but the darkness surrounding him offered no details.

"Hello?" He swallowed hard. "Is someone there?" His eyes bulged and he didn't blink as he hoped to catch a glimpse of whatever was near.

A second, more pronounced thump in the opposite corner made Alister jump to his feet. "OK," he said, his heart hammering inside his chest like a thousand feet stomping, "you're scaring me. Maybe I'm not ready for this." His legs trembled and his throat felt dry. He rubbed his arms against a sudden blast of cold that caressed his flesh.

Unexpectedly, the door to the room he occupied opened, and light from the hallway beamed inside. Alister squinted against the sudden brightness and tried to focus on who or what might have opened it. Suddenly, the front door to the house opened and slammed shut with such force trinkets on tabletops and inside display cabinets rattled.

Running out of his room and through the house, Alister paused only long enough to open the front door. Sprinting to the sidewalk, he looked down the street both ways and only saw the regular flow of traffic.

A vehicle came to an abrupt stop in the northbound lane, halting traffic in that direction. Alister watched the driver, a young woman, exit her vehicle and train her eyes on him. She crossed over the southbound lane without yielding to traffic and stopped before Alister.

"You've been heard," she said, and she smiled. Her eyes appeared unfocused and her actions seemed controlled. "I hope you're ready for this."

The young woman turned away from Alister and faced her car. She looked over her shoulder toward Alister. "The shit is about to hit the fan." She stepped off the curb and hurried into the southbound lane. A passing vehicle struck her, throwing her into the air. Tires squealed and Alister watched the woman twirl without control until she smashed onto the windshield of a stopped northbound vehicle. Blood poured from ripped flesh, and the unfocused look in her eyes became everlasting.

A wave of screams erupted like lava exploding from a volatile volcano. People stepped out of their vehicles and inspected the woman with unblemished horror. Alister remained on the sidewalk, the shouts became background noise as he tried to understand what had just happened. The reason behind the bizarre tragedy should have been obvious to him, but the idea that he'd gotten death's attention overshadowed his logic.

Present day.

"I'm hungry," Alister said to Anna. She had just entered his room, and he watched her move to the chair by the window and sit.

"I promise you will eat soon enough," Anna said. "Have you been given enough time to cool off?"

"I was hoping you'd leave me strapped to this bed and not feed me. Then I can prove that what I tell you about the curse is all true."

"Don't be ridiculous," Anna bit back. "I'm your doctor, not death incarnate, and certainly not someone willing to starve someone to try and make a point."

"You know I won't starve. You won't—"

"Let you? It turns you into this hulking zombie that doesn't stop until your necessities are met?"

Alister looked away. "You make it sound silly when you say it like that."

"Because it is silly, Alister. That's been my point." Anna searched her pocket and came out with a bottle of pills. "And I know you know that, and I can't understand why you resist the truth."

"Most of the things you tell me are nothing but your truth. They don't mean anything to me."

"No," Anna said firmly. "They are your truths, but you're unwilling to face them. Do you not want to get better?"

"No," Alister said as he struggled against the leather straps that bound him. They rustled as they pulled back, and Alister quickly gave up the fight. He allowed his body to sink into the mattress. "I know my memories are real."

"No," Anna said. "They're not. It's time you let them go."

"I can't," Alister said. "They're a part of me."

Anna shook the bottle of pills she held. The contents rattled loudly and held Alister's attention. He held his head up off the pillow. "I need you to take one pill every day. If you skip a dose, I will have it administered. They will help control the hallucinations." Anna placed the pills down on the windowsill.

"I'm not hallucinating," Alister said. "I would like to ask you for one thing," Alister said as he attempted to chase an itch on his scalp. The restraints didn't budge. "I have an itch."

"Where?" Anna asked, and she moved to Alister's side.

"Above my left ear," Alister said, the desperation quickening his words.

Anna scratched where Alister requested. "I'm assuming this wasn't what you wanted to ask for? What is it you'd like to ask?"

"I would like you to take me to see the director or bring him here. There are a few questions I would like to ask him."

"What do you want to ask him?"

"I want to know if he blames me for the death of his friends and if I've ever been sick."

"OK," Anna said. Anna stood and moved toward the door. She opened it and said, "Bruce, can you undo the patient's restraints and escort us to the director's office?"

"To the director's office?" the voice coming from the hallway said. The voice was deep.

"That's right. The patient has requested to see him, and I cannot find reason to deny that request."

Bruce entered the room. He stood tall and wide, and he breathed heavily. A strong smell of sweat and garlic followed him and quickly overtook the room.

"Now, don't you try and give us any trouble," Bruce said, and he unbound Alister's hands and legs.

"I'm not looking to," Alister said as he rubbed the impressions the straps left in his flesh. "I just want to see the director."

Alister stood behind Anna, and he could hear Bruce wheezing close behind him and smell garlic mixed with sweat. The smell was like a toxic assault designed to attack the senses. This reminded him of the officers gagging as they weaved through the pile of garbage inside his darkened house.

Anna knocked on the door and backed up a step, grinding her heel into Alister's toe. Alister groaned, and Anna quickly lifted her foot.

"I'm so sorry," she said, and the director shouted for her to enter the room. She turned her attention to the door and, as instructed, she entered the small office. Bruce stepped in front of Alister, and Alister followed him inside.

Director Conroy sat at his desk buried behind a stack of papers. His eyes peered over the mound focusing strictly on Anna. "Dr. Lee," he said, sounding pleased to see her. "How is the progress with Alister coming along?"

"Well," Anna said with a hint of reluctance, "that's why I'm here." She reached behind Bruce and took hold of Alister by the arm. She pulled him forward and said, "He requested to speak with you."

The director slowly stood and appraised Alister as he walked from behind his desk. Alister kept his eyes trained forward, hoping the director would lose his cool and throttle him for all his loss.

"I can't tell you how happy we are to see you up and about," the director said with a wide smile. "Dr. Lee has been reporting all the progress you have made."

The director pointed to a chair positioned in front of his desk. "Please," he said, "have a seat."

Alister wrestled with his confusion and the idea that his memories were not reality. He looked to Anna for an answer, but she was looking back at him for the same thing.

"Go ahead and sit," she said. "This is your chance to ask any questions you might have."

"Questions?" the director asked, looking to Anna. He turned his attention to Alister. "You have some questions for me?" He moved to his seat and sat. "I would love to hear anything you might have to say."

Alister looked to Anna and Bruce and returned his gaze to the director. He swallowed hard and tried steadying his nerves. "Do you still blame me for the death of your friends?"

The director looked to Anna then back to Alister. "The death of what friends, Alister?"

Alister shifted in his seat. He began picking at the scarred flesh on his palm. "Your doctor friends and the former director. They all died when I first came here to Sunnyside."

The director shook his head. "No, Alister. I've been the director here for over twenty-five years, and none of my staff died because of you. The director before me retired and now lives in Maine."

Alister continued to explore the grotesque mound of flesh, finding his attention becoming more fixated on the dimples, swirls and discoloration within the scarring. "I suppose you're going to tell me I've been sick before?"

"As in the common cold or flu?" the director said.

Alister shook his head.

The director rested his elbows on his desk and moved his hands as he spoke. "Yes, you've been sick before, but I can assure you it's no more than your average patient. Although we do try and keep the facility as clean as possible, visitors and staff bring germs in from outside."

Alister held his palms out to show the director his scars. "Can you tell me how this happened?"

The director looked over Alister's shoulder where Anna stood. The director returned his attention to Alister. "You chewed them. We had to fit you with a leather device that wrapped your head and cupped your chin. We had to leave that device on you for weeks." The director interlaced his fingers and leaned toward Alister. "Do you not remember having this conversation with me only a month ago?"

Alister shook his head. "No, because I haven't spoken to you ever."

171

"Well," the director said as he sat back, "you've given me that same answer before."

Alister thought about protesting but didn't see the sense in it. There was a certainty that the director would be insistent he was having a hard time discerning real memories from those merely imagined. "Can you take me back to my room now?" Alister said. "I'm not feeling well and would like some time to lie down."

"Would you like to see the doctor?" the director said.

"No," Alister said.

"Bruce," Anna said from somewhere behind Alister. "Can you escort the patient to his room?"

Bruce helped Alister to his feet, and the director stood with him.

"You've come a long way, Alister," the director said with a smile. "You should be proud."

CHAPTER 28

A DOSE OF REALITY

The vegetation that continued to flourish in the garden held Alister's attention. He pressed his face against the glass and clenched his jaw.

"It'll never last."

"What won't last?" Bruce asked. He had escorted Alister to his room after meeting with Director Conroy.

"Everything being so alive outside." He moved away from the window. "It is all going to brown again, and that will force Anna to cover my window."

Bruce pursed his lips, shook his head and looked away. "You should try and get some rest."

Alister sat in his chair. "I'm not tired." He crossed his legs. "I'm curious to know why I've never met you before." He folded his hands in his lap and looked at Bruce with a forced smile.

Bruce made no attempt to hide his amusement. He moved to the window and pointed toward the bench in the garden. "I think we've seen each other before. I believe I waved hello to you from over there, but you ignored me."

The memory widened Alister's eyes. "You were the guy in the garden digging holes for the plants." He stood. "But you're a patient."

"Don't be silly, Alister," Bruce said. He walked to the door, opened it and stepped into the hallway. He looked left and right and turned back to Alister. "You have no idea how crazy you sound sometimes."

The door closed, and Alister listened to Bruce's laughter fade. He moved to the bed and, lying prone, he began to count out loud. He planned to stop when he reached a thousand. Tired of the lies and constant confusion, he decided the best way to get the truth was by becoming proactive.

Alister extended his count to fifteen hundred before he got out of bed and moved toward the door. He peeled away the corner of the paper that covered the small window and scanned what little he could see of the hallway.

"It is time to get some answers," he said.

Confident the hallway was unoccupied, he pulled the door open enough to fit his head through. He looked left and right, and everything was clear.

He drew a deep breath, stepped into the hallway, paused and listened. The complete silence kept him still. No moans, no screams. No doctors or orderlies moved about.

There should be screams, shouldn't there?

He trudged forward and settled in front of a door directly across the hall from his. Cupping his hands around his eyes, he peered into the small pane of glass. The contents of the room were almost identical to his. It had a small table pushed against the wall, a twin-size bed and a chair positioned in front of a window. There was an obvious outline of a person that sat in the chair and remained still.

Alister raised his knuckles to the door and paused. "No," he said, and he lowered his hand.

He turned away from the door and started to walk down the hallway.

"Keep your thoughts straight."

When Bruce had escorted him back to his room from the director's office, he was determined to memorize every turn, fire extinguisher and numbered room.

"Now let's see how good my memory really is."

When he arrived at the director's office door, Alister didn't hesitate. He twisted the handle and pushed the door open. The lights in the room were off, and the closed blinds allowed slivers of horizontal beams of sunlight bathe the director's desk in a blinding brilliance that cast eerie shadows. Director Conroy was seated behind his desk, facedown with arms spread wide on the desktop.

"Director Conroy?" Alister said. "May I have a moment of your time?"

Tap. Tap. Tap.

The director didn't stir, and Alister edged toward him.

"Director Conroy?"

Tap. Tap. Tap.

He paused.

Tap. Tap. Tap.

Alister crept closer still.

Tap. Tap. Tap.

A stream of blood that came from the director's nose stained his upper lip and glistened in the strange light. Alister stood over him, unsure what to do.

Tap. Tap. Tap.

"Where is that coming from?"

A small pool of blood that surrounded the director's head brought Alister close to the director, to his knees and then underneath the desk.

Tap. Tap. Tap.

The blood dripped off the desk and into an open drawer that held a book. Alister took possession of the book and inspected it. It was old and smelled that way, too. The overstuffed binding was split and pages hung out, unattached.

"You shouldn't be out of your room."

Alister jumped back and dropped the book. Newspaper clippings, photos and other unidentifiable contents spilled out onto the floor. He turned toward the door with wide eyes, and the powerful thump of his heart hammered inside his chest.

"You need to return to your room and pretend you never saw this," Michael said. He closed the office door.

"Is she making you do this?" Alister said.

The sweat reflected off of Michael's head, and his skin was so pale he appeared to glow in the dark.

Alister picked up a photograph that had fallen out of the book and held it in the light. It was his precious Becca wrapped in a towel. Her lips were blue and her eyes partly open. "It's all true, isn't it?"

"It is." Michael took a step forward. "And she warned me not to talk to you about it. She has my wife and daughter."

Alister saw that same desperate expression staring back at him once before. It was in the mirror the day he placed the gun in his mouth and it misfired.

"She's evil," Michael said. "She's going to torture them."

Alister examined the photograph and saw his wife lying in a pool of blood, her wrists slashed. He looked away from the photo. He leaned against the desk and tried to catch his breath.

"Has she begun to kill again?" Alister said.

Michael looked over his shoulder, his focus toward the door. "Keep your voice low. I don't know where she is, and I don't want to think about what will happen if she finds us in here with him." He gestured toward the director.

Alister dropped the photograph. "The killings?" he asked. His teeth showed and a sudden surge of defiance helped him stand upright. "I want you to tell me everything you know about the killings or I'll start shouting. I swear I will."

The past.

Compressors rattled loudly and made the floor vibrate. Michael leaned against the wall to rest his hip, which thundered with pain. The intense heat of the boilers working to warm the entire hospital brought sweat to his brow, and the smell of oil was strong. He covered his mouth and nose with a handkerchief.

"Michael do this, Michael do that," he said as he shined a flashlight on the low hanging pipes and made his way to the compressors. He examined the machinery as he hobbled by it, looking for obvious signs of a malfunction. A leak, smoke, fire, anything that might tell him in his limited knowledge that there might be a problem.

"Now I'm a maintenance man, too. Why don't they get themselves a replacement when he goes on vacation?"

He came upon a boiler butted against Terry's makeshift wall. A cool breeze touched Michael's arm, and he shined his light down the tunnel, which consumed it.

"I hate it down here."

He swept the light back and forth, forgetting the pain in his leg for the moment. Jumping back, he saw that Terry was lying on the floor face up with his legs folded under him toward his torso.

"Terry," Michael said as he shined the flashlight over him. He didn't see any visible injuries, and there wasn't any blood. He squatted next to Terry and tried to roll him flat. His body was stiff. Michael scrambled to his feet and shuffled toward the exit.

"Slow down," Anna said. She descended the steps and settled on the bottom stair.

Michael turned and pointed toward Terry. "It's Terry. He's on the floor, and I think he's dead."

"Oh, he's dead." Anna shook her head. "Everyone thinks he's away on vacation." She smiled. "I would like to keep it that way."

Michael looked toward Terry and then turned back to Anna. "I don't understand. We can't just leave him there." He started to step past Anna.

Anna stood in front of Michael. "Think about what you're doing," Anna said. "I would hope you wouldn't get in my way after I've been so nice to you."

"What are you talking about?" Michael's brows wrinkled. He pointed at Terry. "A man is on the floor over there dead."

"Yes, he is," Anna said. "And it's because of me."

"What do you mean because of you?"

Anna moved off the bottom step. "It's exactly as I said. I did it."

Michael pushed himself past Anna, his eyes wide with fear. He struggled up the steps.

"Michael?" Anna asked, and he stopped. "I wouldn't do that if I were you."

Suddenly his knees buckled, and he grabbed at a sharp stabbing pain that came from somewhere deep in his gut.

"I don't think you want to know what I'm doing to you," Anna said. "It is merely a show so you know that I'm not fooling around. I am who Alister says."

"Please," he begged, gasping. "Make it stop and I'll do whatever you need."

And like a switch being flipped, the pain disappeared. Michael sucked in a deep breath and sat on the top step. He felt his abdomen and couldn't find any pain. He wiped the sweat from his brow and looked at Anna. Her hands were clasped behind her back and she stood by the makeshift wall.

Michael forced himself to stand, and he went to her. Anna held out her hand, and it began to steam.

"The hot air is interacting with the coldness of my skin. After all, when one is dead, their skin does not generate heat." She moved her hand to her side. "Alister seemed to have picked up on this right away."

"How..." Michael said, fighting all the questions. "Why?" He lowered his chin. "I don't understand."

"I've come to claim my prize," Anna said. "Because if someone can show me that much affection, then what they have to offer must be limitless. I have been around since the creation of life, and I have never experienced anything like it. I won't let it go. Not ever."

"But why do you have to kill?" Michael said. "He is yours to take if that is what you want. I won't stand in your way."

"Everyone's life is mine to take. It is what I was created to do. To kill." She smiled, and it quickly faded. "Don't take what I've come to do personally. Think of it as business."

Michael swallowed hard. "And what have you come to do?"

"Create utopia," Anna said. "Do my bidding and live. Cross me one time and your wife and daughter will suffer immeasurably. Not a word to anyone."

Michael nodded. "Where do we fit into your utopia?"

Anna smirked, turned away and started up the metal steps. "That depends on you and your level of cooperation."

Present day.

"That is how the killings began," Michael said. "I'm sorry I didn't believe you." He began to cry. "But how could someone ever hope to understand what you claimed to be true?"

"Who did she tell you she was?"

Michael shook his head. "She's death incarnate, Alister, and you are her prize."

Alister swore he felt his heart stop, yet he continued to live.

The past.

"I want you to go home and get your wife and daughter," Anna said to Michael, and she turned away. "You have one hour to make it there and back. If you deviate from my instructions at all, you will be introduced to a heart attack." She clasped her hands behind her back, whistled and started to walk away.

"Oh, wait," she said, spinning on her heels. "I should warn you, though. I've begun to make my utopia, and there are few who will live long enough to see it." She pointed to the clock on the wall. "Hurry along. Your hour starts now."

Michael looked at his watch.

Ten o'clock.

He hurried from the hospital. His handicap kept his ability to move quickly at a minimum. Minutes later, he got into his four-cylinder economy car wishing he had a Porsche. Starting the engine and throwing the gear into drive, he stomped down on the gas pedal and the front wheels skidded. The car raced out of the parking lot and onto residential streets.

Vehicle accidents littered the roads and dead bodies were scattered as far as the eye could see, dropped wherever they were when death struck. The devastation was surreal, like watching a horror film. He tried not to notice details but couldn't muster the will to look away.

Michael had to slow down as the maze of cars tightened. He weaved in and out of tight paths, and a vehicle that had run headlong into a telephone pole stole his attention. Its hood was crinkled, its windshield cracked and steam bellowed from the front end. The driver's head was bloody and pushed into the steering wheel. His weight engaged the horn, causing a constant blare.

The man slowly lifted his head and looked at Michael. "Please, help me." Flaps of flesh hung from his face, and his wounds bled in a thick, oozing stream.

Michael trembled and shouted out. "Damn it." He clutched the steering wheel and slammed on the gas, and the small car collided with stalled vehicles, bouncing off them as it carved its way out of the metal and rubber graveyard.

The rearview mirror showed the increasing distance Michael placed between himself and that man, and he barked his displeasure of having to do that.

Michael turned on the radio and tapped the program button in search of a distraction. Every station had static.

"My God," Michael said as he turned the radio off. He concentrated on maneuvering around clusters of stalled cars, and he tried to keep his focus away from the people that ran after his vehicle. Their screams of desperation made his skin crawl.

Michael directed the vehicle toward his lawn and pounded the brakes. He tried to run into his house but could only manage a hurried wobble.

"It's Michael. Where are you?"

A distant horn blared, a house alarm wailed and the desperate shouts of those near and far away distracted him.

Michael climbed the stairs. He tried the bathroom door and it was locked. "Open the door. I've come to get you out of here."

His wife opened the door. His daughter stood behind her. She held a large knife.

"I don't know what's happening," she said, and her body shook. "People have been running around in hysterics. They're dying out there."

Michael eased the knife out of her hand and set it down on the sink. "Come," he said, and he picked up his daughter. "We have to get away from here." He looked at his watch.

10:33.

He directed his wife down the stairs and to his vehicle.

"Is this some sort of an attack?"

"I'll explain along the way," he said. He shielded his daughter from the chaos. "Keep your eyes closed, baby."

His wife climbed into the back seat and lay prone. Michael placed his daughter next to her. "Keep your heads down, and don't look up no matter what you hear." He closed the door behind them.

"Michael," his neighbor Ralph said. "Thank God you came home." He ran over to Michael. Blood leaked from his ears and stained his shirt. "There's something wrong with Linda. You've got to help me."

"There is nothing I can do for you, Ralph. I'm sorry." He rounded the car and opened the driver's door.

"Please!" Ralph said, and he grabbed his arm. "Help me get her into your car. We can take her to a doctor."

"Have you looked at yourself?" He shrugged off Ralph's grip. He looked to his wife and daughter, who continued to hide in the back seat. "You're in no better shape than she is."

"She's suffering terribly and the phones aren't working. You've got to help me."

"I can't," Michael said as he attempted to get into the car. Ralph yanked his arm. The force threw him to the ground. The flesh on his knees and elbows ripped open.

"We've known you for over twenty years, and this is how you treat us?" Ralph kicked Michael in the ribs. Michael gasped.

"I'll kill you, you bastard!"

Michael struggled to his feet, balled his fist and, with all of his might, swung it into the center of Ralph's face. With the sound of a crack, Ralph yelped and fell flat on his back.

10:41

"I'm sorry, old friend," Michael said as he tired to shake the sting from his knuckles. "But I have to worry about my family."

Michael jumped into his vehicle and sped toward the hospital, uncertain if he had enough time to make it back.

Present day.

"I can't take much more," Michael said, and he sat on the floor with his back against the wall. "I'm so damn tired."

Michael's eyes were so puffy and red that Alister didn't know how he could see out of them. "How long ago did this start happening?"

Michael looked to Alister from somewhere far away.

"Michael? When did this first happen?"

"I can't even think. I just need to get some sleep."

"I need you to answer my question."

"I don't know." Michael opened his hands. "Three, maybe four days ago. The days started blending together, and she won't let me sleep."

Alister knelt beside Michael. "What else does she have you doing?"

"Clearing the hospital grounds of the dead."

"How many?"

"I think she got all of them."

Alister stood and ran taut fingers through his hair.

"She put together a group of people that begged for their lives. She made them work."

"Doing what?"

Michael shook his head. "I don't know, mainly removing dead plant life outside your room. Then she made them put in living plants. That is when she took you outside."

Alister paced the floor. "I knew it."

Michael looked at the director's lifeless body and slapped his hands over his ears. "The sound of his blood dripping off the desk is driving me crazy."

Alister forced Michael's hands away from his ears. "She's going to kill you like she did everyone else. Get yourself together."

"I can't," Michael said. "I don't have the energy. Just let me sleep for a while."

"No. We need to kill her; it's the only way."

Michael shook his head. "We can't kill something that is already dead."

"She's vulnerable," Alister said. "She had to give up something to come here, and I think I know what that is. I can't do this alone."

Michael rubbed his eyes. "OK." He drew a deep breath and stood. "What do you need me to do?"

"I need you to distract her."

"OK." Michael nodded his head and swallowed hard. "But don't forget she has my wife and daughter."

CHAPTER 29

STALLING TACTICS

Alister looked at the simulated scenery outside his window. He poked a stiff finger off the glass as he spoke. "What I see is a bunch of plants that are alive, and I know they were dead before you boarded my window."

"Alister," Anna said as she shook her head, "think about what you saw while you were outside. Everything was alive."

Anna moved close to him and he turned so he could see her out of the corner of his eye. He didn't like the idea of her standing behind him. Her nearness had changed from a feeling of comfort and acceptance to one of danger and concern.

"I feel the heat from a flame that doesn't burn." He looked at her and widened his eyes in anxiety. "That is what you've come here to tell me, isn't it?"

Anna blew out a gentle sigh. "Let us not harp on the same subject over and over."

"Don't patronize me," Alister said. "You put a patient in an orderly's uniform—"

Anna reeled. "A patient in an orderly's—"

"—I could smell the smoke from the fire on his clothing."

"There was no fire."

"Ah, so there it is." Alister nodded. "And that must mean there weren't any bodies being burnt either."

"I can bring Michael so you can question him if you'd like."

"Don't bother."

"I would leave the room if you somehow thought I'd sway him."

"He would still lie because you kill people and he's probably afraid of you."

Anna pointed to herself. "I kill people?" She shook her head. "That's ridiculous." She started for the door. "I'm going to get Michael."

"And I told you not to bother."

Anna turned to Alister and opened her arms wide in question. "What would he have to gain by lying to you?"

Alister folded his arms and leaned against the wall. "You don't get it. It's not a question of what he would have to gain by lying but rather what he would have to lose by telling me the truth."

"How can I defend myself against your accusations?"

"I could see his fear," Alister said. "I had that look once, and it was when I first realized I'd gotten your attention."

"This conversation has gone from silly to absolutely ridiculous."

"Why aren't you scribbling down any notes? Am I cured or have you finally given up on me?"

Anna's eyelids fluttered. "We're running around in circles here. We'd made such terrific progress, but lately we've regressed. I'm disappointed."

Alister smiled. "Should I apologize?"

"I'm disappointed in myself, not you. I told you when we first started this things would be trying and there would be certain things you'd have to confront that would challenge you. This includes facing your delusions, the conspiracy theory you have running around inside your head and the loneliness you have to endure when I'm gone. And just because I'm not taking notes doesn't mean I've stopped listening or that I've given up on you."

"I think that was the make-you-feel-bad speech." He turned his back to her. "I still say you're hiding something. I'm interested in meeting the hospital staff. All of them."

"I'm not going to bring you around anyone while you're acting like this."

"And there it is again," Alister said, and he made the sound of a bomb dropping. "Boom! The perfect reason to keep me here and far away from finding the truth."

"You're completely unreasonable today."

"You know something?" Alister kicked off his slippers and got into bed. He looked away from Anna and settled on his side. "I'm done talking."

"Don't shut down on me like this, Alister. We need to talk through this."

Alister closed his eyes and fought the urge to retort. The knowledge that she would eventually leave if he kept quiet ruled.

CHAPTER 30

ON THE MOVE

Alister crept into the hallway, his eyes immediately drawn to the door across from his. Curious if the occupant had fallen victim to Anna, he pressed his forehead against the window and peered inside. Though encased in shadow, he could clearly see someone still occupied the room. He was sitting in the chair perfectly still with his back to the door.

Alister raised his knuckles to knock on the door but decided to try the handle instead. The door opened with a slow, protesting creak. Every muscle in his body tightened and his eyes concentrated on the figure in the shadows.

The person did not move.

Alister breathed a sigh of relief and tiptoed into the room. The darkness within swallowed him, and the bed and table reminded him of the mounds of garbage that lined every room in his home. The powerful smell of feces and urine forced him to hold his breath.

Lost within the shadows, Alister stumbled over something and fell to his knees.

"Who's there?"

Alister jumped to his feet. A slow tingle moved down his spine and stilled his feet. He looked at the chair, and the shadowy figure stood next to it.

"Who are you?"

He was tall.

"What do you want from me?"

And wide.

"Why don't you speak?"

He lunged toward Alister. Enough light seeped into the room from the hallway so that Alister could see his features.

"Bruce, it's Alister."

Bruce stopped and looked over his shoulder toward the chair. "Bruce is here?" He knelt on the floor and looked beneath the bed. He stood and pointed at Alister. "Are you hiding him from me?"

Alister shook his head. "No."

"If I get my hands on him, I'll kill him. And if you're hiding him from me—"

"I'm not."

Bruce stepped forward and stood nose to nose with Alister. "Are you looking for trouble or something?"

"No."

"That's good," Bruce said, and he returned to the chair and sat. "You should know Bruce is extremely dangerous. If I were you, I'd be careful with him."

Alister slowly exited the room and pulled the door closed. He bent at the waist and grabbed his knees. "Holy shit." The surge of adrenaline made his legs wobble and shortened his breath.

Something slammed into the door from inside Bruce's room, and Alister recoiled. Bruce's face was pushed against the small pane of glass, and spit ran from his mouth in a thick wad. His eyes were ablaze with panic.

"Please get me out of here," Bruce said. "Lester's in here and he's after me."

Alister ran down the hallway, through double doors and down another hallway. Each turn he made appeared identical to the last.

Lost and wheezing, Alister slowed his run to a walk and tried to figure out his approximate whereabouts. He pondered how many rights and lefts he'd taken.

He was lost.

A black sign with white letters at the end of the hallway caught his attention.

"Medical," he said, smiling.

CHAPTER 31

PROTECTION AGAINST EVIL

Alister stood in front of an illuminated glass cabinet that housed a perfectly arranged assortment of liquid medications.

He leaned forward and read the typed font on a label on one of the bottles.

"Thiothixene."

He smiled.

"I know you."

He pulled the handle, but the door was locked. He turned away and hit the glass with his elbow. Jagged pieces fell to the floor with a crash.

He grabbed a vial and inspected it further. A rubber membrane stretched across the top of the small, clear bottle. This prompted him to search through cabinets and drawers until he located syringes. Taking one, he pushed the tip of the needle through the rubber casing and into the liquid and pulled back on the plunger until the barrel was full. He capped the needle, put it in his pocket and exited the medical room. Looking down the hallway both ways, indecision kept him still.

Distant, echoing shouts had nearly escaped his notice. He leaned forward, straining to decipher which direction they were coming from.

Closing his eyes, he focused.

"That way," he said, his eyes opened wide and aware. He ran through long corridors, navigating lefts and rights as if he knew the layout. The further he traveled, the louder the shouts grew, and that encouraged him to run even faster.

The hallway dead-ended at an employee cafeteria. The swinging doors were chocked open, and long windows that went from the ceiling to a two-foot cement wall divided the cafeteria from the hallway.

Alister pulled himself close to the wall and tried to control his breathing. He was certain the shouts had to do with Michael, and if he were going to offer him help, he would have to gather himself. If he were to rush inside without insight, he wouldn't be doing either one of them any good.

Alister took deep breaths and blew them out through pursed lips. On the wall opposite him, painted portraits of former hospital directors stared at him. The late Director Lofton looked stern and critical of Alister being out of his room.

He got on his hands and knees and crawled along the floor, employing the short cement wall as cover. Just a few feet shy of reaching the cafeteria door, a shrill stopped his advancement, confused his courage and roused his fears.

His taut fingers tried to grasp the cement floor, and he searched the hallway behind him.

Empty.

A distant memory that didn't form fully made his body tremble and forced a whisper from his mouth.

"Mother."

He didn't know why and tried to remember.

"Look at me when I'm talking to you."

Alister clamped his eyes shut and braced himself for a smack.

"I told you to look at me."

He didn't want to, but something inside told him he should.

"You dare defy me?"

The words came from the cafeteria.

His fears were calmed by a curiosity so strong that it compelled him to peek over the wall.

He ducked back down, his heart hammering inside his chest. He fought the compulsion to flee.

"I want to hear your fear," Anna said, her voice loud. "I need to feel your terror."

Alister looked over the wall again. Anna stood in the center of the room, and a bloody, beaten woman begged for her life at Anna's feet.

"Say it like you mean it, and I might let you live." Anna kicked and punched the woman. Alister cringed as he watched, unable to look away.

The woman took the blows, one after the other, without guarding herself.

"Don't you give up on me," Anna said. "You die only when I'm ready to let you die."

Anna paused in her assault and pointed at someone across the room. Alister followed her finger and saw Michael with his daughter. He held her close and shielded her eyes from Anna.

"Please," Michael said, "I've done exactly as I was told."

"Tell her not to give up on me," Anna said.

Tears streaked Michael's face. "Get up, baby, please. You have to be strong."

Anna looked at the woman. She was still.

"She's weak, and I don't believe a word you say," Anna said. She wrapped the woman's hair around her wrist and pulled upward. "He isn't convinced the stories he's been told are real."

Anna drove the woman's head downward with a stomp and her face smashed into the ground. A dull, meat-smacking thump echoed throughout the room, and a spray of blood stained the floor.

"And that," Anna said, pointing at Michael, "is because you told him something you shouldn't have."

Michael knelt and protected his daughter in a hug. "I didn't. I swear."

"You swear?" Anna laughed. She looked to the woman and said, "Die."

The woman convulsed and gurgled.

"No," Michael said.

Anna walked toward Michael and he moved his daughter behind him.

"Not behind you. Over here," Anna said, pointing to the floor by her feet.

"Don't do this."

Anna turned toward the woman again and said, "Live." The woman's eyes flicked open as she gasped and choked, and blood oozed from her mouth.

"How many times she experiences death depends on your ability to listen. Bring your daughter forward."

Michael encouraged his daughter to stand where Anna had instructed.

"I don't want to go to the bad woman," the young girl said. She cried and remained where her father placed her.

"You have to, baby," Michael said. "Just for a little while."

The woman continued to gasp and spit blood. The little girl looked at her mother and then back at Anna.

"Please help her."

"Do you believe your father is telling me the truth?"

"Yes."

"Well, I don't."

The little girl started to sob.

"Can I have my mommy back?"

"Maybe," Anna said. "Your answers depend on it. If you were to lie to your parents, what would they do?"

"They would be mad with me."

"Is that all?" Anna smiled and stroked the girl's head. "It's OK to tell me everything. I won't let them do anything to you. Not anymore."

The little girl looked to her father. "But I don't want you to hurt them."

Anna knelt in front of the girl and took her hand with a firm yank. The girl whimpered.

"You need to tell me if they got mad at you, what would they do to you?"

"They would hit me and send me to bed without any dinner."

"Just hit you?"

"Beat me," the girl said, and she looked to her father. He stared at the floor and muttered incoherently. She looked at Anna. "They would make me wear long clothes so people wouldn't see the bruises."

"They would do that to you?" Anna said. She kissed the girl's head, stood and walked to the woman. "But you're just a child." She helped her stand.

Anna looked to the girl. "How much of that can you take? How long until you've had enough and fight back?"

Anna picked the woman up by her throat until her feet dangled off the floor and squeezed.

"No more," Anna said, and she twisted her wrist. The neck bone snapped, the sound forced a scream from the little girl, and Michael fell forward and cried.

Anna looked at Alister. "Can't you see that I can protect you against those who might do you harm? I can help make you strong."

Alister leapt to his feet and ran through the corridor until he no longer had the stamina to carry on.

Bent over at the waist with his hands on his knees, he struggled to catch his breath. A peculiar noise coming from a darkened room caught his attention. He approached with caution.

"Hello?"

The door was open, but the light from the hallway didn't penetrate the darkness.

Hack.

Alister moved away, wary not to walk into a trap.

"Is there someone there?"

Hack.

The sound had an element of distress, and Alister pushed his apprehension aside and moved forward. He peered inside the room and could see the silhouette of a man hanging from the ceiling by his neck. The person flailed, gasped and reached out for Alister.

CHAPTER 32

THE THING INSIDE

Alister ran into the room and grabbed the man by his legs. He tried to lift him to take some pressure off of his neck.

"Try and loosen the noose," Alister said. He gave it everything he had to hoist the man higher, and his limbs trembled under the strain. He grunted and started to lose his grip.

"Please," Alister said, "I can't hold you much longer."

"It's too late for him," Anna said from outside the room.

Alister's tired limbs wanted to agree, but his will defied it. He wasn't going to give up and hand her another life. "Help me," Alister said. "I can't hold him much longer." He staggered but regained his balance.

"It's OK to let him go." She slipped her hands into her pockets. "We're much better without him."

"No," Alister said, and he growled as he lifted the man higher. "I won't let him die. You've taken too much from me, and I won't allow you to take any more."

"But you don't understand what you are trying to save." Anna flipped the light on. "Look at him and tell me you want anything to do with him."

Alister looked, gasped, let go of the man and tripped as he backed away. The man that hung flailed and the noose tightened its hold, forcing the veins and eyes in his head outward.

"You see that now, don't you?" Anna said. "Despicable."

A gurgle trapped inside the man's throat kept Alister's attention.

"That was the side of yourself that was once good," Anna said.

The hangman's face was bright red and desperate with pain and fear.

"Your need to care is what makes you vulnerable."

"Is that—"

"Worry not. It's only a part of you," Anna said. "The part you have no use for."

"Please God, no."

"I hung him there to make him suffer as he has made you suffer."

"How has he made me suffer?"

"By trying to take away everything I've ever done for you."

Anna exited the room.

A war scream that startled Alister filled the hallway and turned Anna askew. Something moving so fast that it was nothing more than a blur slammed into Anna and took her out of sight.

"Run, Alister!"

Alister recognized Michael's voice. The desire to help the man that dangled by his neck made him hesitate.

"Now," Michael said. The sound of an intensifying scuffle grew louder.

"I can't leave him," Alister said, and he jumped on the hanging man. Something on the ceiling groaned and snapped and together Alister and the hanging man fell to the floor.

Alister jumped to his feet, loosened the noose on the man and ran from the room. Michael and Anna continued to exchange blows. Michael's handicap seemed no longer visible.

Alister moved forward while he planned his attack, knowing this might be his only chance.

CHAPTER 33

WHAT MUST BE DONE

Anna straddled Michael's chest and cackled. Without pause, she delivered a fist, one after the other, into his face.

"Get off of me!" Michael said as he bucked, twisted and flailed his limbs. Swollen welts and gashes leaking blood distorted his appearance, and Alister could instantly see the man was really a boy no older than the age of eight or nine. And Anna was really the child's mother relishing in the fear and pain of her son.

"Get off of him," Alister said. His words were no louder than a whisper, and he was paralyzed.

"You little bastard. You don't know how to listen!"

"Get off of him," Alister said, his words building but still a whisper.

"I hate you! Do you hear me? I hate you!" Anna said.

Past the physical damage, Alister knew the boy's spirit was being crushed and transformed into something terrible. It seemed inevitable that he would grow up to be an outcast and become an abuser himself. Another participant tangled in the web of hate.

"Can't you see what this is doing to him?"

Alister wanted to take the boy in his arms and carry him someplace safe. It was a place no one knew about and where wounds would be given enough time to heal. Beneath the long, hulking branches and thick canopy of a weeping willow awaited shelter and protection like the hug from someone who cared.

Alister charged forward and lowered his shoulders. He slammed into Anna, and she was thrown off of the boy. The force of the impact jolted Alister's system and stole his breath.

"You dare?" Anna asked, already on her feet. "After all I've done for you?" The surprise of his attack contorted her features.

Alister gasped for air, his lungs on fire.

"You need to sit," someone said.

He struggled to his knees.

"Calm down. Your breath will come soon enough."

Alister fell forward on his hands and tried to draw a breath.

"Raise your hands over your head." The voice was male and the care it seemed to have for him was genuine.

"Like at this, Alister." He demonstrated by lifting his hands over his head.

Alister looked and stopped.

"You."

The man next to him smiling and speaking softly looked exactly like him. He was reminded of the face that used to look back at him in the mirror. It wasn't the one obsessed with the thought of suicide and death that held onto misery but the one that liked the way his hair looked when he ran a comb through it.

"You look like me."

The man chuckled and slapped Alister on the back. "Yes, I suppose I do."

Alister continued to study the man. The physical similarities were endless.

"I knew you would find me, Alister. Thank you." He tugged on the collar of his shirt and Alister could easily see bright red rings around his neck that oozed something terrible.

"You were the one hanging in that room," Alister said. The realization pushed him to his feet. "Who did that to you?"

"I think you know." The man covered the wound and turned away. "She's gone for the moment but could return any second. We should take advantage of the opportunity to get away from here before she returns."

"Where would we go?" Alister balled his fist and held it out. "I think we should stay and fight."

"No. Fighting her like that is doing things on her terms. There is another way."

Alister followed the man into a room, and the noose he had pulled the man down from dangled from the ceiling again.

"I thought that came down when we fell to the ground," Alister said.

The man slid a chair beneath the noose, stopped and looked at Alister. "It did." He patted the chair. "Please, have a seat right here."

Alister sat.

"Give me the syringe that's in your pocket."

"How did you know?"

The man held out his hand and wiggled his fingers. The lumpy flesh on his palms matched Alister's perfectly. "Please, Alister, we don't have much time."

Alister dug in his pocket and withdrew the syringe. He handed it to the man.

"You need to roll up your sleeve."

Alister hesitated.

"You know what is going on. This is what you've always wanted, isn't it?"

Alister searched deep within for the answer, and there was never any doubt about it.

"Yes. Yes, it is."

"Then you need to follow my instructions without pause. Pull up your sleeve."

"I'm not afraid to die."

"Yes, I know because neither am I."

The man squeezed the plunger on the syringe and stopped when a stream of liquid shot out of the needle tip. "How about pain? How do you feel about that?"

Alister rolled up his sleeve and looked away.

"No more pain. I've had enough of that."

"Yes, we have."

"We?"

"I think you know, Alister. You got this needle and filled it because that was what I suggested you do."

Alister flinched at the small stab of pain and looked to see the contents of the needle being pumped into his arm. "No, I took it with the intention of using it on Anna."

The man shook his head. "You brought it here for me to use on you. Although we're different in many ways, we're both in search of the same ending."

Alister raised a brow.

"Anna isn't who she says she is, and she's not who you think she is." He sat next to Alister and paused long enough to touch the oozing lesion on his neck. "It is important for you to know that she's the one responsible for keeping me away from you. I escaped the darkness once, but she caught me, bound my hands behind my back and forced me into the noose. I've been hanging there for days, unable to free myself and get back to you."

"And who or what are you?"

The man smiled. "Your ability to think logically."

Alister laughed. "That's ridiculous."

"I was once a part of you, and we were separated long ago."

"By what?"

"Cruelty."

Alister looked at his hands and flexed his fingers.

"I've been trying to get back to you for a long time. Now that I have, you know what we must do now, don't you?"

Alister nodded. "I do."

"I knew you would." The man turned away. "The woman who calls herself Anna. She is really our mother."

"How..."

"Something inside us brought her out, and she's been inside here," he said as he tapped his temple, "wreaking havoc ever since. She created this hell for us and plays on our fears, desperate to keep us apart."

"What hell?"

"This place—it is only within our mind."

"Why didn't you come and warn me sooner?"

"Oh, I tried, but it was almost impossible to get you to hear me. Especially when she returned to you the second day."

Alister thought of the hospital and how big it was. He had spent most of his days trapped inside that little room, leaving everything else for Anna.

He laughed.

No, not Anna. It was his mother. He had allowed her to run free.

"I eventually started getting through to you, and that's the reason you started to question her."

"I couldn't imagine what you were going through."

"When I would start making progress with you, she would distract you with another lie. Every time she left your room, she would hunt for me. When she eventually caught me, she locked me away deep within the scars of our mind. And she knew each scar intimately because she created every one of them."

"That is where we are now," Alister said. "Caught inside the trappings of a sick mind."

"And there's only one way out for us."

Alister embraced a moment of silence.

"She told us we were worthless," Alister said. "We were beaten every day for nothing. We suffered to satisfy her sick mind."

Alister took hold of the man's hands and turned his palms upward. "I remember now." He compared the scars one last time and let go of his hands. "She did this to us."

"We had many great years with our family while we were able to keep control over her. I think it's time we regained that control."

Alister looked away. "It's fuzzy, but I think I remember them, too. He's been here recently, hasn't he?"

"Yes, he has."

"Does he know?"

"Who, Michael?"

"Yes, Michael.

"That he's our son and that we love him? That we're sorry?"

Alister nodded.

"Yes, he knows that. When we worked together as a team, we were able to tell him."

"I am glad. He deserves that much." He began to cry.

"No more crying."

"OK," he said, and he wiped the tears. "I hate her for what she's done to us."

"I do, too."

Alister stood and slipped his head into the noose. "Finally, we can have peace."

"Alister!" Anna said. She stood in the doorway and was drenched in sweat and short of breath. "What are you doing? Come down from there."

"No," Alister said. "I won't listen to you anymore."

"You're sick and don't know what you're doing."

"No, Mother, you're sick, and you've infected me. To know I've allowed you room inside my mind to carry out your evil sickens me."

Alister stepped off the chair and kicked it away.

"Alister, no!"

PART II

REALITY

CHAPTER 34

LAST SACRIFICE

Bonnie hummed softly. The sound of her sneakers squeaking in the emptiness of the hallway kept perfect time with the simple melody.

"No, no, no," she said, and she stopped walking. The tray she held had a large bowl of water in its center that swirled and spilled over the rim. The other items on the tray—a towel, a bar of soap, a toothbrush and a tube of toothpaste—got wet.

"Damn," she said, and she stomped onward less careful with everything now that it was soaked. When she arrived at a closed door, she balanced the tray in one hand, keyed the doorknob and pushed the door open with her shoulder.

"OK, Alister."

She stepped into the room; the door slowly swung closed behind her.

"I've come to give you your bath."

Although Alister had never responded to the sound of her voice in the ten years she had fed and bathed him, Bonnie believed he heard every word she said and that he appreciated it.

"It is a beautiful day outside today."

And that one day he would say something back to her.

"The doctor told me you responded to the sound of your sons—"

The tray fell out of Bonnie's hands and crashed to the floor. The water drenched the floor, walls and Bonnie's legs.

"Oh my God!"

Her hands covered her mouth and muted a scream. She backed away with her eyes wide and transfixed on Alister's limp body swaying on a makeshift noose torn from the innards of his mattress. His face was blue, and his head was titled at an awkward angle.

Bonnie backed into the wall and slipped. Her tailbone crashed on the hard floor and her head snapped back and slammed into the wall. Stars filled her eyes, and a surge of pain tensed her body.

She moaned as she struggled to her feet and winced as she moved. She looked over her shoulder at Alister and quickly looked away. She pulled his door open and shouted out into the hallway.

"Help! Somebody, please help!"

CHAPTER 35

A LIFELONG COMMITMENT

Anna wiped away her tears with a tissue and looked to Director Conroy's closed office door.

"I don't want to go in there." She sniffed. "Not now."

Her gaze moved to Jennifer, Director Conroy's secretary. She was on the telephone speaking low enough not to be heard. Her desk was to the left of his door, and nobody got past her unless she approved. She handled everything from his phone calls to his appointments and always made sure he had enough coffee to keep him going.

"I'll let the director know you were here, Dr. Lee," Jennifer said. Her hair was in a ponytail and it swayed with the movement of her head.

"Thank you."

Jennifer smiled, and Anna continued to watch her. She was a Barbie doll—pretty with a body to die for, which she showed off with her tight-fitting suit-skirts. But Anna couldn't figure out how because she sat all day long behind the desk. Her butt should be as flat as a pancake and her belly decorated with a few rolls of fat.

"The director is ready for you," Jennifer said, her words prompted Anna's heart to pound.

"Thank you." She stood, grabbed her briefcase and tried to steady her legs. She drew a deep breath and slowly blew it out. "I can do this without crying."

"What?"

Anna shook her head. "Nothing. I was talking to myself."

Anna entered the director's office, and he was standing behind his desk. A concerned look creased his brow, and his eyes were fixated on her. He offered her a seat with an extended hand.

"Please."

There were two nailhead leather chairs in front of his large mahogany executive desk. The chairs were angled slightly and stiff to the touch. The quality was meant to impress family members of patients as well as investors.

"Thank you." She chose the chair to the director's left because it was closest to where she stood.

"Can I get you anything?"

"No, thank you." She placed the briefcase on her lap. She popped the locks and gathered files. She held them out for the director to take. "You will find everything is in chronological order. I've included all prescribed medicines and treatment methods as well as a detailed log of the interactions we had. If there are any questions with my treatments and or diagnosis, I will be more than happy to offer the board an in-depth written or oral presentation."

"Thank you, doctor," the director said as he sat down. He placed his elbows on the desktop and leaned forward. "You are always very thorough. Your accomplishments with the Kunkle patient haven't gone unnoticed. I'm sorry for the loss."

Anna's eyes welled with tears. She looked away and choked back a whimper.

"I know I don't need to ask if you're going to be OK," the director said, and he handed her a tissue. He sat back and studied Anna.

Anna tried to fight the tears away, but they'd become relentless. "I'll be fine," she said.

The director smiled. "I'm going to give you two weeks off, full pay. I want you to take that time to gather yourself and come back fresh."

Anna wiped her tears and looked at the director. "I appreciate that. I really do, but—"

The director shook his head with resolution. "Forget it, Dr. Lee. I'm not taking no for an answer. You're taking the time off and that is it."

"But I have so much work to do."

"I said forget it."

"There are other patients that rely on me, and I know how close I am to a breakthrough with them."

The director rocked in his chair and clasped his hands together. He rested them on his chest. "Your patients and work will still be here when you get back."

Anna sighed. She knew she could lose herself in her work, but at home the silence would allow her plenty of time to mull the signs she had missed along the way—signs that might have saved Alister's life.

"I know how much you cared for Alister, and his death was a terrible tragedy," the director said.

"Maybe I pushed him a bit too hard."

"Don't question yourself like that. It's not fair. You're a good doctor. You need time to mourn the loss."

Anna looked away. Her bottom lip quivered.

"If you find that you need more time than that, just let me know."

Anna shook her head. Her tears tasted salty. "He was a good man, and I think I was beginning to get through to him." She looked at the director with reddened eyes.

"You achieved great results with the patient, but you should know how sick he was more than anyone."

Anna sniffed. "I can't get away from the feeling that I missed something. There had to be a sign along the way. Maybe if I had spent more time trying to figure out what he was trying to say."

"Even you have to sleep sometime, Anna. You should leave here today knowing you provided him with the best care possible."

"Should I?" Anna shook her head. She closed her briefcase and locked it. "I still believe there had to be a sign somewhere along the way that I missed. And that thought is going to haunt me for a long time to come." She stood. "Thank you, director. I appreciate you talking with me."

The director stood. "You call me if you need anything." He lowered his chin. "And I don't want to see you here for two weeks."

Anna exited the room. The surprise of Alister's death followed her out the door and continued to walk with her stride for stride. Alister had shown signs of moving outside the arcane madness of his mind. He had acknowledged his son, asked how his wife was and even wondered where he was. It was like something inside his mind shut off, and he was only able to turn it back on for a minute—just long enough to say good-bye to his son.

"Dr. Lee?"

Anna withdrew from her reverie and faced the voice that summoned her. Michael, Alister's son, stepped forward and hugged her.

"I wanted to thank you for everything you've done for me and my family," Michael said.

Anna was speechless. She failed him and here he was, thanking her. His regard for her filled her chest with a tangible ache.

"Normally people don't care enough about someone like my father. But you put forth effort and I never doubted your concern," Michael said. "I know all that abuse he took as a child had something to do with what he did as an adult. But because of you I got to spend one last moment with my father and not that monster that lived inside his head and made him kill my mother and little sister. I wanted to let you know that all of your hard work over the years has given me one last joy I will never forget. I believe he was able to step out of whatever world he had created for himself long enough to say good-bye to me. You've given me something positive I can take with me for the rest of my life. I have peace knowing that the good side of my father was still in there fighting to get out."

Michael placed a gentle kiss on Anna's cheek, and she watched him walk away through eyes that cried for both her successes and failures.

EPILOGUE

ABUSE

The past.

Young Alister was in his backyard engaged in play. He ran a toy car through mapped-out streets carved inside his mother's rock garden.

He imagined he was a police officer in a high-speed car chase. Two violent bank robbers shot at him as he swerved and dodged their bullets. A variety of sounds added to the drama.

"Alister," his mother said. She was in the kitchen and shouted through an open window. "Come inside for dinner."

Alister groaned in protest. "Just when I was about to get 'em." He hopped to his feet and got a whiff of the homemade meal.

"Meatloaf," he said. It was a guess. "And mashed potatoes." He moved with haste. The growl in his stomach was sudden and painful. "Corn and some gravy."

He brushed the dirt off his pants and ran to the back door. With eager energy, he pulled open the screen door, and the hinges whined.

"Wash up," his mother said. She was still in the kitchen.

"OK." He headed toward the bathroom.

"What the hell are you doing?"

Alister froze and cringed. He looked at his mother. Her eyes were bright with rage and her hands were on her hips. She held a dishtowel, and an apron was wrapped around her body.

"Is it too difficult for you to wipe your feet before you come inside?"

Dirt footprints trailed behind him.

"You don't think, do you?"

The dishtowel whipped him and he flinched. The fabric end snapped like a giant rubber band. He yelled and jumped back. The sting instantly throbbed.

"Don't you dare move away from me, you disrespectful little bastard!" She whipped him again. "Do you think I clean all day long just so you can screw it up?"

"I'm sorry," Alister said, raising his hands in defense.

His mother moved nose to nose with him and pointed in his face. "Lower your hands."

Alister complied.

"Why can't you be courteous and wipe your damn feet on the mat outside instead of on my floors? Does my hard work mean that little to you?"

"I'm sorry. It won't happen again."

"You're sorry?"

She cocked her fist back, and Alister took a step away.

"What are you so afraid of?" she said. "You're a wimp. Now get a towel and clean up your mess."

Alister went to step past his mother and she shoved him. He fell to the floor and hit his elbow on the way down.

"What in the hell is going on in here?" his father said. His speech was slurred and his legs wobbled. A half empty beer bottle occupied his left hand and a lit cigarette sat loosely between his pointer and middle finger in his right hand.

Alister rubbed his elbow.

"I'll tell you what's going on," his mother said. "Your son has been in the house for two seconds, and he's already gone and screwed things up. Everything I've worked on today has already gone to shit."

Alister stood. His elbow pounded with pain.

"Damn kid," his father said as he took a drink.

"Well, he's the bastard you wanted, so you deal with him," she said, and she threw her towel down. "I can't keep going through this day after day. That boy is going to be the death of me. I swear it."

"Alister," his father said. He teetered and finished his beer.

Alister backed away.

"And now look," his mother said. She removed burnt food from the oven, dropped it on the stovetop and slammed the oven door shut. "Dinner is burnt." She stomped off.

His father lunged forward and slapped Alister on the back of his head.

"Ow!"

He pinched the skin on the back of his arm and twisted it.

"Now I have to listen to her all night long. Now clean up after yourself and go to your room."

Alister rubbed his arm. The pain in his elbow was gone.

Alister watched his father go to the refrigerator and grab another beer. He collided off walls as he retreated to a room in the back of the house.

"I'm leaving," Alister said, but he dared not say it too loud. His mother might be around, and the last thing he wanted to do was get her angrier than he already had. "And I'm never coming back."

He got on his hands and knees and cleaned the floor. The thought of his departure was squashed by the painful memory of his mother standing over him. Spit flew from her mouth as she screamed how useless he was and how he would never amount to anything.

"She's right."

Where would he go?

"Nowhere," he said, and he wanted to cry but didn't dare.

He wasn't allowed to have any friends, and he barely knew his way around the neighborhood.

"I'm stuck here forever."

He returned the cleaning supplies to their proper places.

"Alister?"

The hair on the back of his neck stood up. That was his mother, and it sounded like she was upstairs. He walked to the bottom of the steps and looked up at her.

"Yes, mother?"

"You do understand there will be no dinner for you tonight?"

"Yes," he said. "Father already told me."

"Good."

Her voice was calm, and her hands were behind her back.

"I cleaned up my mess," he said. "I was going to my room."

"Come upstairs for a minute. I would like to have a word with you."

Alister hesitated but knew he had to go. He kept a watchful eye on her as he climbed each step. She remained still and revealed nothing in a blank stare.

He arrived at the top step and kept his hands by his side.

"Yes, Mother?"

"You know once I decide on a punishment, I can't go back on it."

Alister nodded.

"Because if I do, that makes me weak and a liar, and I am neither."

"I know that, Mother."

"And you understand what you did was wrong?"

Alister swallowed hard. "I disrespected the hard work you did for me and Dad."

"You meant to say Dad and I?"

"Yes, Dad and I."

"Very good, Alister. I'm sorry."

He wavered. "Thank you, Mother."

She sighed. "You really don't understand, do you?"

Something inside told Alister to move away from his mother, but he resisted it. He knew if he were to move without being dismissed, it would only provoke her.

"I can't keep going through this; I feel like I'm on the verge of a nervous breakdown."

She swung something shiny and heavy out from behind her back, raised it over her head and pulled it downward, aiming it at Alister's head.

Alister raised his hands to deflect the blow. The tip of a clothes iron crashed into his hands. Skin, cartilage and bone were damaged, and he screamed. He lost his footing and tumbled down the stairs. The wall, ceiling and stairs whipped past him as he painfully pounded each step.

His momentum halted when he hit the landing. His hands hurt and flaps of bloody torn skin hung open like a gutted fish. Something that rumbled down the steps caught his attention and forced his eyes wide. He saw his mother skip steps two at a time, bounding down after him.

"Get up," she said. "You're bleeding on my floor."

Alister jumped to his feet. A sharp pain that stemmed from his hip nearly toppled him over. But he fought the pain and ran out the back door.

"Get back here, you little bastard!"

He heard her shouts but ignored her. The instinct to survive didn't allow him to look back.

More than three hours had passed since young Alister ran away from home. The darkness of night had placed a blanket over the day. The tree he sat beneath was hard and the ground lumpy. His hip throbbed, but nowhere near as bad as his hands did. The bleeding had stopped, but a constant sting he wanted to scratch was within the patch of mangled flesh. It was difficult to look at, and when he did, it hurt worse.

"I'm hungry," he said in response to the growl of his stomach. He shivered at the chill that crept through his clothes, and every sound around spooked him.

"I have to go back home."

Maybe, he hoped, his mother had gone to bed and his father had drunk himself to sleep. He would be able to sneak into the house and wash his hands beneath the faucet that had a slow drip. He would crawl into bed and try his luck tomorrow. Maybe things would be better with his mom and dad if he didn't screw up all the time.

But no matter what he believed, he would always be a victim of his parents' evil, and that would only breed his malice—malice he would struggle to contain as he tried to have a family of his own.

26684751R00126

Made in the USA
Charleston, SC
16 February 2014